DEMON DANCE AND OTHER DISASTERS
A SPIRIT MAGE'S JOURNEY

BR KINGSOLVER

Demon Dance and Other Disasters

A Spirit Mage's Journey, Book 1

By BR Kingsolver
https://brkingsolver.com/

Cover art by Lou Harper
https://coveraffairs.com/

Published by BR Kingsolver

Copyright 2024 by BR Kingsolver

LICENSE NOTES

This book is licensed for your personal enjoyment only. All rights reserved. No part of this book may be reproduced or transmitted in any form or by any means now known or hereinafter invented, electronic or mechanical, including but not limited to photocopying, recording, or by an information storage and retrieval system, without the written permission of the Publisher, except where permitted by law.

In ebook or other electronic format, it may not be re-sold or given away to other people. If you would like to share this book with another person, please purchase an additional copy for each recipient. If you're reading this book and did not purchase it, or it was not purchased for your use only, then please return it and purchase your own copy. Thank you for respecting the hard work of this author.

Get updates on new book releases, promotions, contests and giveaways!
Sign up for my newsletter.

ACKNOWLEDGMENTS

My deepest thanks to Heather, Fatima, and Valentina for their help and insights. The book is much better due to their inputs.

CHAPTER 1

I had spent two weeks tracking Madeleine du Mont—a three-hundred-year-old vampire with a shocking disregard for the covenant between her kind and the Mage Guild. The streets were deserted due to a deluge of rain that had started that afternoon and continued into the night. Madeleine must have been hungry, or maybe vamps that old didn't care about the weather.

My guess as to where she was spending her days had turned out to be right. A basement apartment in an old building south of Capitol Hill. No way could I break in there during the day, so I had waited.

She set out in a direction I didn't expect. Her usual hunting ground had been out on East Colfax, taking either the hookers or their clients. Low-hanging fruit, which indicated to me that she was lazy. With the cold rain, there probably wouldn't be much business going on there, so instead, she was headed toward Cherry Creek, and probably the night clubs and strip joints.

Vampires were fast, but she didn't seem to be in much of a hurry, so I didn't have any trouble keeping up with her. And with the rain as hard as it was, I didn't worry much about being quiet. I doubted even she could hear anything softer than thunder.

I caught up with her when she hit the creek, which was more like a river then, with the rain adding to runoff from the snowmelt in the mountains. The park ran alongside the creek, with Speer Boulevard on the other side. If she was headed where I thought, she would have to cross the creek, and that meant finding a bridge.

Casting my personal shield, I drew my katana and a wooden stake from my bag, then moved to close with her. My suppositions about her hearing were obviously mistaken, as she stopped at the end of the bridge, spun around, and laughed.

"Are you to be my dinner tonight, little mage? I haven't had mage blood in weeks."

She sprang, covering the ten or fifteen feet between us in a single leap. I braced, and held the sword out in front of me, but she dodged it and slammed into me. Even with my shield, the force of her knocked me down.

My shield frustrated her, as she couldn't get a grasp of me. I wriggled free, but she wrapped her arms around my legs, and I fell again. She was too close for me to use the sword, and she avoided the stake. Usually, my shield gave me an advantage against the bloodsuckers, but Madeleine was faster and stronger than any opponent I had ever faced. I dropped the katana and drew my wakizashi—a short sword, or a long knife. Much better for close fighting.

Madeleine backhanded me, a blow that I felt even through my shield. She had to have felt it, too—like punching a brick wall—and hesitated. I turned the tables and rushed her. She stumbled on the wet, uneven grass, and stepped backward to regain her balance.

My knife slid into her belly with barely any resistance, and I saw shock on her face. The wound wouldn't be fatal, or even disabling, but I hoped to get an opening to use the stake.

Madeline turned her body, and the stake skipped off her arm. I tried to use the leverage of the knife still imbedded in her to keep her from moving away from me, but she pushed me hard with both hands and fell backward. She was too close to the low stone wall at the edge of the creek, which hit her at mid-thigh. I saw her wildly waving her arms, trying to regain her balance.

She fell into the water and disappeared, then surfaced briefly downstream and went under again. Vamps can't swim, and they do need oxygen, so they can drown. I thought I saw a glimpse of her farther downstream, and then there was nothing except the churning power of the water rushing toward the plains.

My father's wakizashi, one of the few things I had to remember him, was gone.

※

I had to stoop to enter the low door, and the rain that had gathered in my hat brim spilled onto my shoes. No big deal, they were soaked anyway.

It was pitch-black outside, so it took no time at all for my eyes to adjust. A few dim lamps on the walls and at either end of the bar made it difficult to tell if I knew any of the people sitting around the small tables scattered across the floor. I knew that the ambiance—if you could call it that—was purposeful. Nick's Cellar probably didn't look much different than it had a hundred years before, although now the dim lights were electric instead of gas or oil.

I made my way across to the bar and put out a five. "Ale."

The bartender poured my drink and swept the money out of sight when he placed the mug on the bar. I picked it up and looked around for a place to sit. A small table with two chairs in one of the corners caught my attention. A good spot where I could sit with my back to the wall.

They called it mud season up in the mountains—the time when the snow melted, and spring rain turned everything into a soggy miasma of shoe-sucking mud. It all washed down to the city at the mountains' base, changing the river running through town into a brown, roiling animal, ready to drown any creature foolish enough not to respect it.

Madeleine had made that mistake, venturing too close and underestimating her opponent. I replayed the look of shock on her face as she lost her balance and fell in, and I wondered how far she would travel before her body washed up on a shore.

It was a problem, since I had no proof of her death. And without proof, the Guild was unlikely to pay. Two weeks of tracking and spying, and then a fight that left me bruised and sore, and with nothing to show for it. I wondered if maybe I should find another profession. Working at the Gilded Lilly next door wasn't a job I relished, but Lilly said I was comely enough, and I could make good money. Perhaps, but I couldn't drum up any enthusiasm for the gig.

Not for the first time, I thought about going back to school. The university would train me for something more socially acceptable than slaughtering vampires and other monsters. I could sit in a nice, warm office building and add numbers until I completely lost what little sanity I had left. Of course, I would have to finish high school first, and I had to eat while I played student.

Or I could apply for an apprenticeship with the Guild. Some of its members had shown interest in me, although some of that interest wasn't welcome. The look in Master Rathske's eyes made it plain that accepting his mentoring meant sharing his bed, and I couldn't imagine that. At least at Lilly's, I wouldn't be stuck with the same unpleasant man over and over every night. But the men would probably have Rathske's tastes, and the same look in their eyes.

Someone moved closer to me, partially blocking the light from the room.

"You look like a drowned rat," Morgan said. He was the only tracker I really considered a friend—although he wanted to be more than friends.

"Feel kind of like one," I replied, not looking up.

"What do you think about a hot shower and a warm, dry place to spend the night?"

I shrugged. "Not really interested in company tonight. I figure I'll have another glass after this one, then find my way home."

"Offer's open if you change your mind." He moved off, back to a table with two other men.

Morgan wasn't a bad sort, and I would be safe with him, but he always made me feel as though he wanted to keep me. It was flattering in a way, but he was twice my age, and there had to be something wrong with a man who wanted to keep house with a sixteen-year-old girl.

CHAPTER 2

It was still raining when I woke up, and the room was cold. I pulled the covers tight around me and sat up. Then I debated whether it was worth it to brave the trip across the room and back to turn on the heat. My stomach growled, and the aching hollow there decided for me.

I pulled one blanket around me, leapt up, and crossed the room in three steps. After lighting the furnace, I raced back to my bed and burrowed into the covers.

It had been a long time since dinner the night before last, and the sausage roll hadn't really filled me up. The two glasses of ale the previous evening were a cruel trick to play on an empty stomach. I had been tracking Madeleine du Mont, who had come to town a couple of months before. She wasn't what one might call a good neighbor, draining her victims and leaving bodies all over the city.

The Mage Guild took a poor view on anything that could bring the shadow world to the attention of normal humans. They put out a bounty on her, an action that led to the deaths of two members of the Guild Council. Madeleine was that kind of nasty girl. The Guild raised the bounty.

A friend of mine, Eric Walsh, had taken the challenge and gone hunting her. His body, drained of blood, had been found two weeks before.

A variety of people, with a variety of skills and talents, became hunters. I had never heard of one younger than me. I collected my first bounty when I was fourteen. My age was a two-edged sword. My quarry usually underestimated me, and I was still growing into my magic and wasn't always sure what I could or couldn't do. I knew I was woefully untrained, and although I had either won or at least survived my encounters, I had been severely battered more than once. It wasn't my parents' fault. My first bounty came from finding their murderers.

Only about half a dozen hunters were successful enough to live off bounties. The rest were more brag than production. I actually made most of my money by tracking lost kids—runaways mostly, but occasionally I found kids who had been kidnapped. I also did skip-tracing for a couple of bail bondsmen, and sometimes found missing spouses and other people for different kinds of lawyers.

The room warmed enough that I couldn't see my breath anymore. That meant there would be warm water to bathe. I reluctantly got up, put a kettle on the stove, and took a shower in the tiny space I could barely turn around in. By the time I finished washing my hair, the kettle began to whistle.

The one-room flat had a small kitchen on one wall, my bed in a nook with a dormer window on the adjoining wall, the miniscule bathroom with a toilet and a shower on the third wall, and the door and what passed for a closet on the other wall. It was in the attic of an old three-story house in a part of town that had seen better days.

I made tea and got dressed while I drank it, then walked out, set the wards on the room, and crossed the landing to the outside door. A set of steep, rickety stairs led to the ground on the side of the house.

A three-mile hike brought me to a much, much nicer part of the city. The Guild Hall—which was disguised as an investment bank—a cathedral, and mansions of some of the more prominent citizens and mages—most built in the early part of the last century—surrounded Carlisle Square. Scrunched in between the imposing buildings were a few shops and cafes. I made for one called the Sunrise Café, which had the best breakfasts in the city for a reasonable price.

I wasn't busted, but unless I scored a nice bounty before the end of the month, I might have to choose between rent and food. Living on the edge was a familiar feeling. Once, I had truly considered taking a couple of shifts at Lilly's, then the Guild put out a bounty on a rogue werewolf that killed a child. I collected his head two nights later and was able to eat. I hated to depend on such events.

When I was halfway through my meal, a man in fine silks stopped at my table. "Miss Dunne? Do you mind if I sit down?"

No one in their right mind was impolite to a senior Guild mage.

"Not at all," I said, gesturing to the chair across from me. I licked my lips, and said, "I hope you don't take this wrong, but I don't recognize you." And I was really curious as to how he knew my real name. I had been named Kaitlyn Dunne, but after my parents' deaths, I went by Katy Brown. Just being careful.

"Master Greenwood," he said. He had a full head of long brown hair and a full beard. His eyes were pale blue, like ice. A hawk nose between high cheekbones gave him an air of dignity. A large man, very tall, and solid like a brick wall.

I certainly recognized his name. Council mages were rather private individuals, and didn't publish their pictures on a website. But one mystery solved. The Guild, of course, knew my real name. All trackers had to register with them to get paid.

I dipped my head. "My honor."

He regarded me long enough to make me uncomfortable, then said, "You've developed quite a reputation. Your father was a friend of mine. I think the Guild made a mistake in not taking you in when your parents died."

I wanted to tell him that he was a couple of years late, but instead said nothing.

"Madeleine du Mont's body washed up downstream this morning. Would you happen to know anything about that?"

With a nod, I said, "She went in the river near Seaton Street."

He held out his hand. My *wakizashi*—my father's short sword—the spelled blade incorporating a silver alloy. I didn't think it would kill a vampire, so she must have drowned.

"Yes, that's mine," I said. "How did you find me?"

He nodded and put it down next to my plate. "I thought I recognized it. You aren't the only tracker in the world. Your father's blade, I believe. You can collect the bounty at the Guild Hall. But there's another issue I'd like to discuss with you. There is a mage—we don't know who it is—summoning demons. As you can imagine, that is of some concern to the Council."

I swallowed. Hard.

"Uh, I'm not sure I'm up to confronting a mage. Especially one with the power to control a demon. Master Greenwood, I'm not trained, and I'm not even sure what talents I have."

"Yes, but I'm not asking you to confront or fight him—or her. Just to find him, figure out who is doing this. We'll pay a generous fee for that information. As to the other, ten o'clock tomorrow morning, 4235 Aspen Way."

He stood, and stayed a moment, looking down at me, then abruptly turned and walked away. I stared at his back with my mouth gaping open like a brainless fool.

The Mage Guild had Guild Halls in most major cities

throughout the world. As part of the Treaty of Krakow that ended the Witch Wars in the seventeenth century, the Guild promised to contain and regulate the use of magic, and the behavior of paranormal and supernatural beings.

If a child had magic—either that of a mage or a witch—it usually began to manifest at puberty. While witches were usually trained by their families or covens, mages were potentially too dangerous to let run around wild. The Guild took charge of training mage children. I had fallen through the cracks, left to try and figure out my magic with no guidance. But it seemed the Master was offering to change that.

CHAPTER 3

The bounty I received for Madeleine wouldn't even buy a good car, but it was enough for me to live fairly comfortably for a year. At least, I could pay my rent and eat regularly for a while.

While I was walking down the street behind a couple of girls my age who were chatting and laughing, a feeling of despondency came over me. God, why did it always have to be so hard? The bounty didn't really change my circumstance, and the whole hustle cycle would soon start again.

After some consideration, I decided that if Master Greenwood was going to take a professional interest in me, I should look at least somewhat presentable. So, I went shopping for clothes. That was rare for me. If it fit and served its purpose, I never cared how an article of clothing looked. I especially avoided anything that might attract the attention of men. So, shopping for new clothes rather than looking for them at Goodwill was unusual.

Master Greenwood didn't give me the feeling that he wanted my body, and that was what a lot of men seemed to be interested in. It was rather funny in a way. I wasn't flat chested, but my boobs weren't prominent, either. The girl in the mirror was pretty, and Lilly said that with proper makeup I'd be a "knockout," so I avoided makeup. At close to six feet, I was tall for a woman, and had shed that gangly awkwardness I had when I was younger. But why men took an interest in me when there were many more welcoming women around was a mystery.

The outfit I chose to go to his home—which was in an area in the foothills that had large mansions with expansive grounds—was a loose dark-blue silk tunic with matching trousers. The tunic was decorated with gold-colored embroidery around the throat and cuffs. The cut was similar to what students at the Guild academy wore, but of a much finer fabric. My landlady, Mrs. O'Reilly, plaited my hair into a French braid. I told her I had a job interview, and she was all in favor of that.

The bus dropped me off a couple of miles from the Master's house, but I was used to walking. At least it had finally stopped raining, though I still carried my new umbrella just in case.

A high wall surrounded the house, and I felt the wards as I walked up the drive and through the gate, but they didn't stop me. There were twelve steps from the driveway up to the front porch. The front door was at least twelve feet high and wide enough to drive a car through. I pulled the cord to ring the bell at exactly ten o'clock.

A butler answered immediately.

"Master Greenwood told me to come," I said.

"Miss Dunne? Come in." He stood aside and closed the door after me. "Please follow me."

He led me to a room that looked a little like a chemistry lab, or maybe an alchemist's lab. The walls were covered with books.

"The Master will be with you shortly," the butler said and left.

"Shortly" turned out to be less than a minute. I barely had time to look around the room before the Master came in with a woman and another man. I had taken time to research Greenwood, although little public information existed. He was the third-ranking member on the Guild Council, well over one hundred years old, and a powerful mage. He had been married at one time and had three grown children, but his wife was dead. He lived with three women—rumored to be concubines, all considerably older than I was—and his household staff.

The man with him looked like a clerk, about my height, balding, and wearing glasses. He wore a brown cardigan over an open-collared shirt and tan dungarees.

The woman was a different matter. She was taller than me, dressed in a tailored lime-green pantsuit with matching heels. She didn't need the three-inch heels, but with them she was almost as tall as Greenwood. Her blonde hair was cut short, and she had a stride and carriage of confidence and power. She looked to be in her early forties, but age was a tricky thing to judge with a mage.

Once a mage reached maturity, magic slowed their aging. Witches and mages lived an incredibly long time, as long as they avoided accidents and conflicts. I suspected that the expected lifespan of trackers probably wasn't very long.

The Master asked me to sit at a table that had a tea service with cookies. He didn't introduce either of his companions, nor did they introduce themselves. The Master sat in a comfortable-looking chair away from the table while the other two sat across from me.

"Tell me about yourself," the woman said. "Everything about your family, your life today, and how you came to be here."

I did as best as I could. I wasn't sure what a normal kid's life was, and what I considered normal had turned upside down when I was fourteen.

"One morning, my parents weren't there, and they didn't come home or call that day. Two days later, a policeman came to the door and told me they were dead. I never got to see them. I was told that my grandparents identified their bodies."

The woman's brow wrinkled, and she leaned forward. "Didn't anyone from the Guild contact you?"

I shook my head. "Other than that visit from the police, the only people I saw were from some bank who came to evict me for not paying the mortgage. They said my grandparents were selling the house."

"Your parents didn't have any money? You were destitute?" It was the first sign of emotion I had seen from her. She appeared to be surprised. "What about your grandparents? Or other family members? Your mother has a sister who lives here in town."

Again, I shook my head. "I haven't seen any of my mother's family since I was about eight. Mom didn't get along with them. The bank told me that since I was a minor, my grandparents took all the money."

The woman glanced back at Master Greenwood, who gave a slight shrug. The other man just sat and stared at me, his expression never changing.

After I told them about my life since my parents' death, and about how I learned to use my tracking skills to earn Guild bounties, they began to ask me about my talents, my training, my skills. One of my father's friends continued to teach me karate and how to use the *katana* and *wakizashi*—long and short Japanese swords that Dad had left me.

Then they began presenting me with various objects. Some they asked me to describe, some they touched me with, or told me to touch.

After about four hours, the butler brought in some lunch— soup and sandwiches—and I asked if I could go to the bathroom.

When we finished eating, I spent another two hours with them asking me to move things without touching them, light fires, raise or lower the temperature in the room, and a dozen other things I had zero idea how to do. Then they asked me to fly, and to turn invisible.

I knew I could glamor myself, but I had always kept it secret. No sense letting that cat out of the bag. But I tripped myself up. I was tired, getting more than a little irritated, so I reacted and became invisible. I didn't realize what I'd done until I saw their reactions.

"Can you glamor me, or Master Greenwood?" the woman asked.

"Can you cast an image of yourself over there?" the man asked pointing across the room.

Damn. "Uh, maybe," I answered.

"Try."

I glanced at the Master. He stared into my eyes and nodded.

I cast an image of myself on the Master, and an image of him across the room, all the while cringing inside. He looked at the illusion across the room, then stood and looked down at himself.

"That is truly amazing," he said, then sat down again.

"Cast an illusion of the riverside park at Speer Boulevard," the woman ordered.

I cast it onto the table between us.

"Recast this room with the doors relocated," Master Greenwood said.

I glanced at him again, then did so.

"But you still know where the real doors are, don't you?" he said, the corner of his mouth twitching with amusement. "A very useful escape strategy. Show my friends your sword."

I took a deep breath, then unglamored the *katana* and laid it on the table. Their eyes widened in surprise, but otherwise they showed no emotion. The Master chuckled.

They sent me away shortly after that, telling me to come back the following day. I wondered what else they had in store for me. After two years of living on my own, growing up too fast, I was skeptical of people offering help. They hadn't told me what I had to gain by cooperating with them, but I couldn't figure out what I had to lose.

I was sure none of the people in that mansion ever considered that the sun was setting, it was cold outside, and I had to walk two miles to the nearest bus stop. I should have worn a heavier coat, but it had been much warmer when I set out in the morning. Besides, in my clothes shopping, I hadn't considered buying a warm coat that would be presentable in polite company. Such a coat was so expensive.

So, there I was, sitting on the bench at the bus stop, when three boys—probably about my age or a little older—showed up. They were acting like idiots, as teenaged boys are wont to do. Partly to show off to the girl, I assumed. But when I didn't react, or flirt with them, they started to get a little mean.

I kept hoping the bus would come, but it didn't before two of them sat down on either side of me and scooted close. Too close, and they got handsy. I didn't want to hurt them, or cause a scene.

"Leave me alone," I said, and started to stand up, but the one on my right grabbed my arm and pulled me back down. I reacted without thinking, turning toward him and slamming the heel of my other hand into his nose. I pulled my right arm free, stood, and whirled around to face them.

The one I had hit had his hand over his face, and there was a lot of blood coming from his nose. The other two stared at me in astonishment.

"I said, leave me alone. I don't want a scene, and I don't want to hurt you. Do you understand?"

I was ready to draw my sword. If they were grown men, I

would have already done so. I'd been in too many situations with people who thought of a young girl as prey. My role was hunter, not prey, and I had shed my inhibitions against using violence years before.

The bus came over a low hill and slowed to a stop. I got on and showed my pass card without ever taking my eyes off the boys. They didn't attempt to follow me.

CHAPTER 4

On the bus ride home, I looked through the folder Master Greenwood gave me when I left his house. It contained information concerning demons and their summoning, with documentation and some photos of what the Guild suspected was going on.

After changing my clothes, I set out for one of the sites where someone had witnessed a demon manifestation several days before.

When I arrived in the alley, the smell of sulfur was so strong I almost gagged. Not sulfur exactly, but an ugly, burnt flavor of sulfur—worse than dog farts. I guessed that was what the report I read called brimstone. I wondered how strong it had been when the demon was present. It was a pretty easy trail to follow. Until I reached a place a couple of blocks from the Guild Hall.

The smell and the presence that I'd been following abruptly vanished. I walked back a few yards and picked it up again, but that was it. The trail evaporated, and casting about in every direction was of no use.

It was getting late, and my stomach reminded me that I

hadn't eaten since lunch at the Master's, so I hit a bar that was frequented by hunters and had decent food. The Tracker Lounge was a couple of steps up in class from my usual dive, and the cook was usually sober.

The bartender took my order, and said, "Congratulations on Madeleine. That was a tough one."

"Uh, you heard about that?" I stammered.

"Largest bounty this year. Word gets around, ya know."

The Guild enforced a bargain with the mundanes—the grand majority of the population. It kept the paranormal and supernatural world in check, meaning that we didn't harass or eat people—or turn them into toads—and they didn't hunt us down and burn us at the stake. It mostly worked, but the bounty system was how the Guild dealt with those who couldn't seem to be able to control themselves.

I took my mug of ale and found an empty table, suddenly self-conscious of people watching me. I had hoped I might be able to sniff out some of the gossip, but if I was suddenly 'a player,' then that would be a lot harder. 'Largest bounty this year.' I hadn't known that. I usually didn't aim for the major bounties, but I felt that my skills were something I could pit against an old vampire. Arrogant, perhaps, but most hunters weren't able to cast a personal shield, not to mention an invisibility glamor.

I set my mug on the table, took off my coat, and draped it over the back of the chair, all the while scanning the room. At least half of the people there were watching me. It made me wonder if I should take a trip to the restroom and sneak out the back door. Surely, no one would think me stupid enough to be carrying that much cash on me.

After a bit, the waitress—a middle-aged motherly type—brought my meal.

"Another ale, hon?" she asked. "Are you all right?"

I nodded. "Yeah, I'm fine."

"If you feel uncomfortable, you let me know," she said. "You'll be safe in the kitchen."

I shook my head. "Thank you. I'm not stupid enough to be carrying that bounty. You don't think...?" I let the sentence hang.

"This is a rough crowd," she said. "I'm Sheila. You're special, Katy Brown, but that doesn't mean you're invincible. I'm not sayin' that someone might try to rob you, but there are men who might feel they need to take a girl down a notch. You understand me?"

I did, and I wasn't in the mood for a beating. I could probably take most of the men one-on-one, but the authorities frowned on killing humans, and taking on half a dozen hunters would be difficult.

"Master Greenwood thinks I'm special, too."

Sheila grinned. "You wouldn't mind if that rumor got around, would you?"

"Whatever keeps me safe."

She laughed, took my empty mug, and headed back toward the bar. I dug into my dinner, and nodded to her when she brought another mug of ale.

While I was eating, I saw Morgan come in, order a drink, then join a table across the room. Shortly thereafter, he turned and looked in my direction, then turned back.

Of all the hunter-trackers operating in the metropolitan area, Morgan's tracking ability was probably second only to mine. I wasn't sure what other talents he had, but he wasn't fully human. He'd grown up in one of the mountain towns, and his parents were guides who took city hunters out to shoot deer, elk, and bear. I think he followed a girlfriend down to the city, and when she shifted her affections, he fell into the Guild bounty system. When my parents died, he had taken me in occasionally. It gets cold on the streets in winter.

The other man who had protected me was Scott Winfield.

Scott owned a dojo—a school for teaching martial arts. He had no magic, but I had taken *katana* and karate lessons from him since I was ten. He was my father's best friend and continued my lessons in karate and oriental weapons after Mom and Dad died. He offered me a place to live when I was kicked out of our house, but his girlfriend said if I moved in, she would move out, so I ended up on the street.

I couldn't figure that out. Scott was like an uncle to me, and I couldn't imagine him being inappropriate. He said that she was weird, and I had to agree. He was in love, and that seemed to make people do strange things.

I had a key to the dojo, and in the worst weather, I had occasionally spent the night in his store room. He helped me get my age-adjusted driver's license and a PI license, and eventually I found the tiny attic apartment.

I finished my dinner and paid my check, then made my way across the room to the table where Morgan sat. There were about a dozen men and women sitting there.

After saying my hellos, I leaned over and, with my mouth near Morgan's ear, asked, "Has anyone run across evidence of a demon?"

He jerked around to stare at me, then shook his head and stood. Grabbing my arm, he dragged me away to a corner near the restrooms.

"Don't be a total idiot," he hissed at me. "You got lucky with Madeleine du Mont, but messing with demons is another level of crazy. Let the damned Guild find their own rogues. It doesn't matter how much they might pay, no one is interested in the job."

"I didn't know a gig was posted for either a demon or a mage," I said.

He shook his head. "There isn't, but you can't have demons killing people all over town and keep it quiet. The Guild is freaking out that the mundane police are going to figure it out and start blaming the Guild." He looked around. I guessed he was checking to see if anyone could hear us. "From what I heard, most of the demon deaths have been mages. Someone is getting even."

I shrugged. "I'm not trying to track a demon. I heard a rumor, and was curious if anyone else heard it. I guess you have."

I made my way to the outside door and slipped outside, adopting a different glamor as I did. People often told me that I looked older than my age, but I didn't think I looked twenty-one. So, I sort of adjusted my appearance when necessary. And that night, in case anyone was waiting for Katy Brown, the woman that walked away from the bar didn't look like her at all.

CHAPTER 5

The following day at Master Greenwood's house, the man in the brown cardigan—no one had yet introduced my interrogators—stuck patches to my temples, the inside of my wrists and ankles, one over my heart, and one on my lower abdomen. Then he hooked me up to a series of machines.

Some of the machines fed electricity to the patches, some seemed to read from them. I got the feeling that some of the machines read magic, because I was asked to try to do certain things, such as cast illusions, while they hovered over the machine's display.

At one point, Master Greenwood threw something at my head. I couldn't see what it was, and wasn't sure whether to try to catch it, duck, or shield. So, I shielded. The orange bounced off, hit the table, and rolled off to the floor. I thought it was a waste of a good orange. I should have caught it.

When we broke for lunch, I drew the Master aside and told him of my attempt at tracking a demon.

"Doesn't surprise me," he said. "Next time, try tracing all the way back in the other direction. When the summoner sends the demon back to their plane, the trail vanishes. But going back the opposite way may lead you to where it was originally summoned."

"You're a tracker," I said. He didn't dispute that statement. "Why haven't you tried to track the mage?"

"I have. At the ritual sites I've found, he—or she—conducted the summoning ritual outside of town, or in one of the larger parks. I've found three places marked for the ritual, but they're isolated, and there's no way to track where the mage went afterward. In other words, I've tracked the demon, but I haven't been able to track the mage. I'm hoping you might be able to."

That afternoon, the Master escorted me to the door and said, "You don't need to come tomorrow. Come to the Guild Hall next Wednesday and ask for me. And if you think you have any helpful information about the summoner, come anytime—day or night—and ask for Dierdre Greenwood."

He handed me a small cloth bag, and shoved me out the door. I waited until I was beyond the wall and the wards before looking in the bag. It contained a ring. Cast with gold and silver, it had clear and red crystals alternately inlaid completely around the band. It was too large for any of my fingers, but fit my left thumb. The note with it said, "It is a focus. Don't take it off."

Okay. A focus for what?

※

I didn't have any new leads, so after I changed clothes, I headed back to the place of the demon sighting I had checked out before. This time, I headed in the other direction. If Master Greenwood had found the site of the summoning, I wanted to see it.

Following the trail of stink was fairly easy. The demon had wandered all over town. I finally reached City Park—an almost-wilderness that covered a square mile in an older upscale part of the city. Most of the buildings surrounding it were built in the latter part of the nineteenth century—between three and four stories each, but not much wider than two of the city buses.

Inside the park, a thicket of aspen trees was shielded from a small pond by a hedge of blackberry bushes. The demon might not have been dissuaded by the thorns, but I was. I cast a shield around me and plowed through to the center of the grove of trees.

There, I found a circle about eight feet across burned into the grass. If I thought the smell of the demon's trail was bad, the stench there almost made me throw up. I wished I could cut off the smell, and almost miraculously, I stopped smelling it. I stopped for a moment to wonder at that. It seemed that I was always stumbling into new aspects of my magic.

It had been more than a week since that particular demon was spotted three miles away. I scouted the area, hoping to find some evidence of the mage who had been there, but I came up empty. Not even a shoe print.

I stood back and mulled that. There weren't any shoe prints at all, even from Master Greenwood or myself. Checking closely, I found a ring of salt marking the edge of the clearing. I stepped outside it, and started leaving tracks where I walked. Inside, no tracks.

So, the mage had created a circle within a circle to summon his demon. Smart, but I knew so little about summoning that someone could have told me anything and I'd probably believe it.

But looking outside the salt circle for prints, I found that there weren't any blackberry brambles on the north side of the aspen grove. Instead, a small finger of the pond curled around, and I found someone's footprints in the mud. Only two or three prints. They were slightly smaller than my boot print.

If I were a bloodhound, the time lag on the prints would

have made them useless. But magically, I could draw their essence and use it. As I did so, I felt the ring on my thumb. It was a weird feeling, not like it turned hot or cold, or put pressure on my thumb. I was just hyper aware of it.

The trail led into the pond. I could guess that the pond had filled and enlarged with all the rain we'd been having, so I skirted it and sought for the trail on the other side. I didn't realize that I'd been practically holding my breath until I found the essence of the person I was trailing.

The sun was starting to set, but I struck out across the park. The trail remained faint but steady. And then I reached the edge of the park, standing on the sidewalk on MacArthur Avenue, watching the traffic whiz by. Two lanes in each direction—buses and trucks spewing diesel exhaust—and the nearest crosswalk a hundred yards away at the light. It was rush hour, and trying to cross where I stood was madness. The trail led straight ahead, neither left nor right. My quarry had crossed there, but I assumed he did it late at night. He certainly hadn't crossed through the rush-hour traffic I faced.

My choices were to continue following that trail, or grab some dinner. Dinner won. The trail was days old, and I couldn't summon any sense of urgency to continue that night. I made sure to identify markers so I could pick up the trail easily, then walked to the nearest bus stop.

CHAPTER 6

The little refrigerator in my flat didn't hold much, and the two-burner cooktop without an oven wasn't conducive to cooking anything elaborate. Not that I had any cooking skills to brag about. But eating out all the time was expensive, and probably not very healthy. The sixty-five-dollar thrift store microwave was a godsend, so I pledged to hit a grocery store soon, and at least get some staples and canned goods that would keep. Meanwhile, I still had to eat.

I decided against any of my usual meal-haunts and went to an Irish pub near the university instead.

As I turned the corner onto the street where Two Fools Tavern was, someone called my name.

"Hey, Katy! Wait up!"

I recognized the voice immediately. Jodi Preston, a street kid two years younger than I was. She had a major crush on me, and if I let her, she'd tag along after me all day and all night. With her auburn hair and blue eyes, Jodi was as pretty as any girl I'd ever seen.

She rushed up and hugged me. "It's been forever!" she said,

breathless as though she'd been running. "I heard a rumor that you took down an ancient vamp! Like, wow! Congratulations!"

Jodi had fire magic, but I wasn't sure how strong it was, and she was completely untrained. The testing Master Greenwood put me through crossed my mind. But unlike me, whose parents were registered with the Guild, Jodi had no idea who her father was. Her mom was a drunk, a drug addict, and a prostitute. Before Jodi ran away, her mom had started selling her. We landed on the street about the same time.

I had sort of lost track of her the previous fall when I found the little apartment in Mrs. O'Reilly's house and Jodi disappeared from the streets. The people on the street were a shifting population. A lot of people took off for California when the weather turned cold.

"Hey, how're you doing?" I asked. "Yeah, it has been a while. You made it through the winter okay?"

"Yeah. Do you know the quilting and knitting shop on Lipan?"

I shook my head. "Afraid not."

"Lady who owns it is Delia Gosling. She lets me stay with her and help around the shop. She's a pretty good cook, too." She turned those huge blue eyes up to me. "Woulda rather been with you." I said a silent prayer of thanks that Jodi had landed with a woman rather than a male pervert.

"Can't do that. My landlady would have us both out on the street, and I have enough trouble feeding myself. But, hey, I got a little spare. Want some dinner?"

We trouped into the tavern. Jodi obviously looked too young to drink, but I told the waitress she was my little sister, and ordered hot tea for both of us. My ID said I was eighteen, old enough to buy beer. In some of the dive bars where I was a regular, they would serve me anything I asked for.

Jodi was definitely gay, but like with most kids living on the street, she did what she had to do to survive. She did look better-fed than the last time I'd seen her. As for me, I wasn't sure what I was—heterosexual, homosexual, asexual. The closest thing I'd ever had to a boyfriend or a girlfriend had been Eric Walsh, who I slept with occasionally, but he had gone and gotten himself killed by Madeleine. Was I in love with him? I didn't think so.

Jodi ordered fish and chips, and I ordered the corned beef and cabbage. We split a bread pudding dessert.

"Has anyone from the Guild ever tested you?" I asked her.

She shook her head. "I stay as far away from the Guild as I can. Some of those mages give me the creeps. They look at me like the guys my mom used to bring home."

I could relate to that, but said, "They aren't all that way. Does Ms. Gosling have any magic?"

"She calls herself a hearth witch, whatever that is. She seems to be allergic to the Guild. Calls them arrogant, but I think some of that is jealousy because they're all so rich."

"Not all of them are rich, but the top levels are, just as the top levels of mundane society are. But they're all certainly arrogant."

We left the tavern, and Jody moved up against me, wrapping her arm around my waist and nestling her head into the hollow of my shoulder as we walked.

"Where's this shop?" I asked. "I'll walk you home." Depending on what part of Lipan Street it was, it could have been not very far from my place.

Jodi stopped half a block away from the shop and pointed.

"That's the shop. I don't think Delia will like you coming home with me. We live above the shop, and there's only one bedroom."

"Take care of yourself. You have a phone?"

She shook her head. I pulled a small notebook from my pocket and wrote down my number.

"If you need me, call, okay?"

She stared at the number, and I knew from past experience that she memorized it in just a few seconds. The kid had a photographic memory and did math like a computer. Then she leapt up, threw her arms around me, and gave me a kiss that sent warm shivers through my body. A fourteen-year-old shouldn't know how to kiss like that.

"I love you, ya know," she said as she backed away.

"I know, kid. Be good and be careful."

I watched her skip away down the street, then turned and headed for my flat six blocks away.

Most of the supernaturals lived side-by-side with the human population, and no one ever suspected their presence. Occasionally a vamp or a were would go rogue, but if there were any serious problems, they were usually from young, recently turned monsters. If they didn't have proper guidance, they could get in all kinds of trouble.

It could be dangerous to take a shortcut through the alleys at night. Staying on the streets under the lights would have lengthened my trip by only a block or so. As I was debating with myself on whether to take a safer route, a young werewolf exploded out from behind several garbage cans next to a dumpster. Maybe she thought that would surprise me and cause me to freeze. It would have worked with most young girls.

I had my *wakizashi* in my hand, tucked next to my body in a fold of my shirt. My stupidity didn't extend far enough as to be totally unprepared. I ducked under her initial lunge, scoring one of her legs with the silver-alloy spelled knife. She screamed like a cat that had been stepped on.

We both whirled to face each other, and I drew my sword while casting the illusion that there were three more of me.

"Bad move," I said. "But if you want to go home and lick your wound, I won't try to stop you."

She snarled and sprang. My sword penetrated under her

ribs. She fell to the ground and jerked, her eyes on my face as the light faded from them.

I watched her form change back to human. She was naked, of course. She looked to be college age, maybe as old as twenty or twenty-one. Long, straight dark-blonde hair. Average height, nice body, although a little soft. I could tell she didn't exercise much before she was turned. And my guess was that she was turned recently. Most rogues who attacked humans were new and didn't have any discipline.

She had a chance to walk away—especially once she saw my sword—and I wondered if she had used me to commit suicide. Trackers told tales of such deaths. Some people couldn't deal with the change and killed themselves. Or they used a tracker to help them. I couldn't imagine what it would be like to know you had a virus that controlled you, and you'd never be human again. A horrible fate.

And if I didn't want to land in jail, or spend a week in a Guild holding cell, I needed to get the hell out of there before anyone came along. The Guild would test her and find the virus in her blood, but I had no idea what the civil authorities did when they found dead monsters.

I spent the rest of my trip looking over my shoulder. I was supposed to be a monster hunter, but obviously I was too stupid to be let out without a chaperone. I heaved a sigh of relief when I got to my room, then cursed myself when I took off my coat before lighting the heater.

CHAPTER 7

In the morning, I set out to pick up the summoner's trail I'd left the evening before. I did find it on the other side of MacArthur Avenue, but it soon led to a tram stop. My summoner had hopped on one of the city's electric trams. Dead end.

The chill in the air from the night before was getting worse. I checked my phone, and the forecast was for possible snow that night, with the temperatures diving well below freezing. That reminded me that I needed to buy a new coat.

Since it was early spring, winter coats were on sale all over town. I ended up getting a ski parka—something I had longed for ever since I outgrew the one my parents bought me. I also bought a nicer coat that was marked down. Definitely fine enough to wear to the Guild on Wednesday.

For the next few days, I bummed around town, sniffing for brimstone, and listening to whatever gossip I could overhear. TV news in a bar mentioned a couple of mysterious deaths the police were very close-mouthed about. A house fire up in one of the canyons was deemed suspicious, and the owners died in the fire.

Other than that, I didn't pick up any clues to possible demon summoning whatsoever.

※

When I turned up at the Guild on Wednesday morning, I was told to sit in a little waiting room near the main entrance. I waited for forty-five minutes before someone came to get me.

The woman was beautiful. She easily could have been a model or a movie star. Even taller than me, she had the kind of natural blonde hair the women reading the news on TV had, and the kind of body that made men drool. It looked as though she'd been poured into her jeans, and the white fitted blouse displayed her flat abdomen and large boobs without showing any skin.

"Kaitlyn Dunne?" she asked as she approached. "I'm so sorry to keep you waiting. I was in a meeting, and no one told me you were out here. Father is out of town, I'm afraid, so you're stuck with me for the day. Come along, and I'll give you the tour."

"Father?"

"Oh, I'm sorry. I'm Dierdre Greenwood. The Master is my father. But I think he intends for me to oversee your training."

She took off down the hall, and I scrambled to catch up with her.

"Training?"

Dierdre grinned. "No one told you anything, did they? Not Father—he tends to overlook such details—and I'm sure Master Olinsky just assumed that he briefed you."

"I don't think I know a Master Olinsky." The head of the Mage Guild was named Olinsky, but I was sure I'd never met him.

"Diana Olinsky. Tall, blonde, corporate type? Blue eyes that look right into your soul? She's head of the Council. I was told she conducted your testing."

I thought I would faint. It was too much. I leaned against the nearest wall, crouched down, and put my head between my knees.

"Are you all right?" Dierdre's voice seemed to come from far away.

Screw it. I just sat down and tried to breathe deeply. After some time, the room steadied, and the light-headedness faded.

"Can you please start at the beginning?" I asked. "No one has told me a damned thing. I'm not even sure why I'm here. Master Greenwood wanted me to track a demon summoner, and that's all I know."

"Ah. Yes, you're coming in through sort of an unusual process. Okay, yes, I can start at the beginning. Are you okay? Do you think you can stand and walk? We can go to the dining room and have a cup of tea, and I'll explain things."

***

"That woman who interrogated me was Master Olinsky?" I asked as we seated ourselves. I had expected something like the cafeteria at school, but the internal café of the Mage Guild was the fanciest-looking restaurant I'd ever been in. A waiter brought us a pot of tea and some cookies.

"Yes. I talked with Dad, and he told me about your testing. The other man was Simon Cartwright. He's a truthsayer. He said that he was surprised at your honesty. No matter how personal the question was, or how badly your answer could make you look, you answered everything truthfully."

"Your father seemed to be offering me a chance. At least, that's what I hoped. I had to trust him. If he threw me out on my ear, I wouldn't be any worse off than I was before. Ms.

Greenwood, I've lived on the streets, and eaten out of garbage bins. Very few people have offered me kindness without wanting something in return."

Her expression softened. "That sounds really rough. Hopefully, you can put all that behind you."

Curiosity was eating a hole in my gut, wondering what Greenwood and the Guild wanted from me. I was sure it wasn't just tracking. But hope was a powerful drug, and no matter how unlikely, I had discovered that the possibility that I might find a place where I belonged made me as giddy as a six-year-old on Christmas Eve.

"That would be nice."

Dierdre nodded. "I assume you would like to know the results of the testing."

I swallowed the lump in my throat. "Uh, yes, please."

"Well, it appears that with training, you might have a variety of talents. We know that your abilities include some air magic—shielding, warding, and illusion. You're a strong tracker, but I think you already know that, and it appears you might have the ability to spell objects. That is something that needs to be explored. I understand that your father was able to do that, and worked extensively with some of our weapons' makers."

She paused, as though trying to decide what to say next.

"Our testing results were a bit confusing. We're going to have to figure some of it out."

"I thought I was pretty useless, except for the tracking and shielding. Hell, I can't even light a match."

Dierdre laughed. "I barely can. But showy magic like fire isn't the only thing that's useful."

She made a motion with her finger, and the water in her glass started spinning like a whirlpool. Her grin was incredibly malevolent as she said, "You could have trapped Madeleine du Mont in the river, instead of just hoping she drowned."

"Uh, what do you do? I mean, here in the Guild. You aren't a teacher, right?"

"Oh, no, not in the standard sense. When did you first get your period?"

I knew why she asked. "I was thirteen. About six months before my parents died."

"So, they gave you some training?"

"My dad taught me how to track, and they both taught me how to shield and cast wards. I'm a lot better at those things now. Practice, I guess."

She nodded. "Normally, children come to us when their magic first manifests. We test them, then assign them to groups with like talents. But you've been learning on your own for almost three years. I'm sure you have some methods and tricks you've figured out by yourself, and some very basic things you haven't discovered."

Leaning close, looking me in the eyes, she said, "I've been assigned to you for two reasons. You're probably not strong enough or creative enough to accidentally kill me, and I'm strong enough to protect the world from you while you're learning. I hope we get along, because you're stuck with me. Maybe a year from now you'll be safe to live and study with other students, but right now, Kaitlyn, indications are that your magic is very strong. You're a potential bomb, and we don't know what might set you off."

CHAPTER 8

"The first thing we'll do is show you your room. You can bring your clothes and other things here. Where have you been staying?"

"I have a flat on the east side of downtown. It's not much, but I just paid the rent until the end of the year. Madeleine's bounty. When will the Master be back?"

"Tonight, I think. If you're going to be demon hunting, you may want to keep that flat for a while. We'll see."

She ushered me into an elevator, looked into a device, and said, "Floor seven." Turning to me, she said, "Retinal scan. We'll have to get you set up with security. You'll have free access to the ground and first floors, the gym and swimming pool in the basement, the portal to the training ground, and your room on floor seven. If you try to go anywhere else, well, you can't. And you'll be able to use the portal only with a senior mage."

I refused to try and take all that in. Simpler to just follow along. I kind of felt the way I did the time someone spiked my drink with LSD. Nothing seemed real.

We walked down a long hall, then turned and walked down

another one. We saw five or six people, all young, but older than me.

Dierdre stopped in front of a door labeled '746', reached out, grabbed my hand, and pulled me toward her.

"Put your hand on that plate. Spread your fingers, and try and make as much of your hand as possible contact the surface. All right, now repeat after me: I am Kaitlyn Dunne. I own this room."

I did as she said.

"Okay, now put your hand back on the plate, and tell the door to open."

I did, and the door slid open.

"When you leave, tell it to lock," Dierdre said, and ushered me inside.

The 'room' was actually two rooms, both a little larger than my flat, plus a bathroom. One room had a double bed, a dresser with a mirror, a chest of drawers, and a wardrobe. The other room had a table and six chairs, a buffet with a small sink, an electric kettle, and a coffee-tea service. There was a small refrigerator next to it—even smaller than the one in my flat. There was also a sitting area with three over-stuffed chairs, a low coffee table, and a television. If I cleared out some of the furniture, I could even be able to practice some kata.

The bathroom held a vanity with a sink, a toilet, and a tub with a shower. It was more than half the size of my flat.

I turned in a circle in the sitting room. "No kitchen?"

"The cafeteria and the dining room are open twenty-four hours a day."

"I can't afford to eat there."

She stared at me for a full minute, then said, "You don't have to pay." She sort of shook herself. "You live here." She pulled out one of the chairs around the table. "They really didn't explain anything to you, did they?"

I guess the expression on my face was dumbfounded enough that she just shook her head.

"Sit down. Kaitlyn, you work here. You go to school here. You live here. Unless you don't want the gig, or you do something so stupid and outrageous that they throw you out, you're a member of the Guild. You have a place to live—for free. You will get fed—for free. You'll get a monthly stipend—about five hundred dollars initially, I think. Possibly more. You're a little different. You'll still get to keep your bounties if you earn any. By the way, did anyone tell you what the bounty on the summoner is?"

I shook my head. "There isn't anything posted. Officially, there is no bounty. Doesn't matter. None of the trackers want anything to do with hunting a rogue mage."

She barked out a laugh. "Too smart. That's probably why Father wants you to do it. Young and stupid. Kaitlyn, I'm sorry, I'm not trying to be offensive, but that's the way I see it. The bounty hasn't been published, but it's a hundred thousand dollars."

I did feel pretty young and stupid. That was five times the bounty I'd collected for Madeleine, and according to Morgan, no one wanted to touch it. I stared at Dierdre and wondered if I should feel insulted, but I didn't. She was just being honest with me. I had a pretty good sense of that. I really was out of my depth.

What I did feel uneasy about was the part about being locked into the Guild without being asked if I wanted to be. I had spent two years on the street, taking care of myself, and being taken advantage of by people older and stronger—and smarter—than I was. But I was learning. I had developed a pretty good feel for when I was about to get raped, whether physically, emotionally, or economically. Sitting with Dierdre, that feeling was buzzing like if I had stuck my finger in a light socket.

Unless I did 'something so stupid and outrageous' that they threw me out—or I ended up dead. She hadn't said that part.

There was an old guy who hung out at Nick's Cellar, cadging drinks and telling wild, incoherent stories. They said he had once been a powerful Guild mage, before he went crazy. The problem with insane mages was that occasionally they destroyed things, and you—or they—never knew what might set them off. What kind of shape would I be in if I lost a fight with a demon?

"Do you need any help bringing your things here?" Dierdre's voice interrupted my thoughts.

The only things I might store in these rooms were clothes, and every stitch I owned would fit in a small suitcase and a backpack.

"No, I'll manage. As you said, if Master Greenwood wants me to track demons, I might want to keep my place for a while. I don't have a car, and most of the buses stop running at midnight. The three sightings he told me about are a lot closer to my flat than here."

Dierdre nodded.

"Can I ward these rooms?"

She cocked her head, and the wrinkles between her eyes indicated that she was thinking about the answer.

"The palm lock is a type of ward," she said after a while. "I guess you can add a personal ward, although I don't know anyone who does that. You know there are mages who can break almost any ward. The only time it might be an issue for us is if you were sick or injured and we needed to get in to help you."

I left it at that. I wasn't sure how suspicious the mages of the Guild were. I thought it was interesting that almost everyone at the Tracker's Lounge thought the summoner was a renegade Guild mage. And at the Guild, they didn't seem to think that. Without any proof, though, I was more than half convinced that the summoner was a Guild mage. It made too much sense. And if I were to get too close to him or her, I could see them coming after me.

Master Greenwood hadn't shown up by nine o'clock in the evening, so I took off. I didn't even have a toothbrush at the Guild, and making my way across town late at night usually wasn't much fun. Sure, I could take care of myself, but anyone who went looking for a fight was an idiot.

CHAPTER 9

I spent the night at my flat, and in the morning, I put most of my new clothes in the suitcase, along with one pair of old jeans, a disreputable sweater, and my old coat. I might want to go out from the Guild as Katy Brown sometimes. The rest of my clothes and personal effects I left at the flat. I hadn't told anyone at the Guild where the flat was, but they were mages, and I had no doubt they could find me if they wanted to.

The ride on the bus was the normal boring midmorning trip. At that time of day, most of the crazies had already settled down in their favorite panhandling sites, and the late commuters were all watching porn or fashion on their phones. I had once lied my way into a mailroom job at a company downtown, but it paid less than waiting tables and was far less interesting.

A woman behind and across the aisle from me shrieked, drawing my attention to her side of the bus. A very large red man—naked, with no hair or tits, so I guessed it was male—was creating havoc while rampaging down the sidewalk. He picked up a woman, who screamed, and bit her head off, which shut her up. That gave me some sense of perspective. The damned thing must have been twelve feet tall.

I had never seen a demon before, but unless he was an illusion, I was ready to be convinced. I scrambled toward the front of the bus, dragging my suitcase with me.

"Let me off!"

"Next stop," the driver barked.

I grabbed his shoulder. "Let me off now!"

He hit the brakes, almost throwing me into the windshield.

"Get off! And don't ever try to ride with me again! I'll call the cops on you, you little bitch!"

We were two blocks past where I'd seen the demon, but that didn't worry me. I ran back down the sidewalk, and almost no one got in my way. There were several injured people lying about, but no one without a head. Many of the shops had broken windows, and quite a few alarms were going off. It didn't look as though the incident would be easy to cover up. And the stench of brimstone was overwhelming.

By the time I passed the headless body, her blood covering the sidewalk, the demon was no longer in sight. Its trail wasn't hard to follow, though. A wrecked car in the middle of the street showed where it had crossed the road, and the mayhem shifted to the other sidewalk.

The wrecked car caused traffic to slow, and I made it across the street without getting hit. The demon had veered into one of the buildings, and I slowed as I passed through an opening framed with mangled metal and paved with broken glass. The inside of the clothing store looked as though a bomb had gone off.

The demon was nowhere to be seen, and there didn't seem to be anywhere that it might have exited. What the hell?

A woman was lying under a table, curled into a fetal position. I didn't see any blood or injuries.

"Are you all right?" I asked, shaking her.

She peeked out between her arms that were covering her face and head.

"I think so."

"Where did it go?"

"I don't know," she said as she sat up. "It just disappeared. What was that thing?"

I didn't try to answer her. I jumped up and sped out of the store to try and track the demon's path back toward its summoning place.

It took me more than an hour—and I all that time I was aware of the ring's subtle work—but the trail led me back to that same aspen grove in MacArthur Park. That struck me as strange. Master Greenwood had told me the summoning locations were all different.

But there was no question the demon had manifested there. The body of the man who had been sacrificed still lay in the clearing.

I had seen a lot of terrible things over the past two years, including a demon eating a woman's head only an hour before. But the stench of brimstone, the look on the man's face, his entrails pulled from his body, and the hole in his chest where his heart had been, were just too much. I dropped to my knees and threw up. Breakfast had been a donut and coffee, but after that came up, I continued heaving, lying on the ground with my eyes closed, trying to block out everything I had seen that morning.

I don't know how long I lay there, but eventually I dragged myself out of the thicket. Pulling my phone out of my pocket, I called Dierdre using the number she'd given me.

"Hello?"

"It's Kaitlyn. Have you heard about the demon?"

"Yes, where are you?"

"I tracked it back to the summoning location. It's at the same place in City Park that your dad told me about."

"We're on our way."

I went back and retrieved my suitcase that I'd dropped when I puked my guts out, then retreated to the edge of the pond. The mage had skirted the pond, then struck out along the same path as I had followed before. I didn't continue following, but sat on a park bench and waited. My tracking abilities involved two different mechanisms. One was a sense of smell that I knew was unusual, and the other was a sense of magic, a sense of a person's, animal's, or object's essence. I really couldn't explain either one, even to myself.

The shock wore off, along with the adrenaline, and I started shaking, hugging myself, and letting the fear roll through me. The look on that woman's face in the shop and on the driver of the car wrecked in the middle of the street haunted me. What would I have done if I actually caught up with the thing? Would my personal shield hold against such a creature?

My phone rang, and after fumbling with it, I managed to answer it.

"Where are you?" Dierdre asked.

"On the MacArthur Avenue side of the thicket. On the south end of the pond."

"Stay there."

A couple of minutes later, Dierdre, her father, and two other men showed up.

"Where did the mage go?" Master Greenwood asked.

I pointed. "There. That's where he went the first time. There's a bus stop. We might be able to figure out which bus or tram he took."

"He?" the Master asked.

I nodded. "I think it's a man. I didn't see him, but the trail doesn't feel like a woman."

The Master told the other two men to clean up the summoning place, and then said, "Lead on."

I fumbled with my suitcase, and tried to stand.

"What's in there?" Dierdre asked.

"My clothes. I was taking them to the Guild."

She took the suitcase from me and handed it to one of the men.

"Take this to the Guild Hall and leave it with Marlene."

CHAPTER 10

We crossed the street to the bus stop, and I scanned the schedule posted there.

"The trail ends here," I said. "The summoner got on a bus, probably route six."

"And where does that lead?" Master Greenwood asked.

I shook my head. "He could get off at the next stop, but trying to figure that out is a mess. If he rode for three stops, there are five different routes that stop at Union Square. But if he continued on route six, it would take him to the Guild Hall. One stop past there, and he could catch the train either south to the airport, or north to the suburbs."

"A very efficient way to throw off any trackers," the Master said.

"What I don't understand is, what was the point? Why turn a demon loose in the middle of the city at ten o'clock in the morning? How are you going to cover this up? I mean, it's like he wants the world to know there are demons."

Dierdre and her father exchanged a glance.

"Or is that the point?" I asked.

The Master sighed. "There are some who feel we should have a different relationship with the mundane world."

He didn't elaborate, and that statement could indicate a lot of different things.

"Have there been incidents in other places?" I asked. "I mean, are things like this happening in Dallas or Los Angeles?" I hadn't heard anything, but I didn't ever see the TV news unless I was in a bar.

He shook his head and turned away. I took that as a 'no'.

"Well, let's get the car and go home," Master Greenwood said.

"Uh, I have some other things to do," I said. Turning to Dierdre, I said, "Is there a time I should come at tomorrow?"

"Come at eight. Ask for Marlene."

"Who is?"

"My apprentice."

"Is that what I am?"

She chuckled. "You're sort of a cross between an apprentice and a student." And someone they weren't sure what to do with.

I watched them strike out across the park, and I took the next bus. I was wearing one of my new outfits, which wasn't appropriate for some of the places I needed to go. With two transfers, I landed a block away from my flat.

After changing clothes, I took the six bus until it hit the police barricades and was detoured. I got off, cast a glamor to disguise myself as one of the city building inspectors I saw on the other side of the barriers, and wandered into the war zone the demon had left.

I spent more than an hour looking at the damage. There was a lot of blood both on the sidewalks and inside some of the damaged buildings. A couple of crews were working diligently to scrub the blood away. There weren't any ambulances around, so I assumed the injured had been taken away. I did see a number of bodies, but the headless woman was gone. Crime scene personnel were assessing the dead, then zipping them into body bags and loading them into vans for the morgue.

The amount of damage was staggering, and people from a city department were checking the buildings, in some cases roping them off and hanging signs saying the buildings weren't safe. In addition to the smashed bricks, metal, and glass, what looked like scorch marks outlined the damage.

And I had dashed after that thing like a complete idiot. Note to self, taking care of myself first—as I had been doing for the past two years—might still be the smartest thing I could do. No matter what kind of shiny things the Guild waved in front of me.

Hunger reminded me that the donut I'd puked up was the only thing I'd eaten all day. I took myself to the Sunrise Café, hoping that due to its proximity to the Guild Hall I might overhear any conversations concerning the morning's events.

The large number of obvious Guild members in the café led me to wonder about the quality of the free food in the Guild dining room. But perhaps it was either a testament to the issue of eating in the same place day after day, or just that the Sunrise had a better cook.

The demon was the subject of almost every conversation I overheard. I sat near the front window, directly behind three men who were obviously high-ranking mages. They were deep in conversation, and didn't even notice me when I sat at a table near them.

"Absolutely disgraceful!" one man said.

"Worse than that," one of the other men said. "It's obviously meant to sabotage us. You heard about the vampire-werewolf public battles in Atlanta and Dallas, didn't you? I've heard speculation that the Knights are behind it."

I had heard of the Knights Magica, a shadowy group of mages supported by the Universal Church. Some people said they were a myth, like the Illuminati.

"Damned stupid," the third man said. "They don't know what they're unleashing. If the mundane humans decide we're more trouble than we're worth, we'll be back to the witch hunts of the Middle Ages. We couldn't hold our own against their numbers then, and there are several billion more of them now."

"I don't care what the Knights might be doing," the first man said. "But summoning demons isn't aimed at giving us a bad reputation. This crap is an attack on us."

They paid their checks and left. I finished my meal and walked out to stare around at the square. The Guild Hall was more than one hundred years old, and had been renovated in the 1930s, then again in the 70s. Or at least the interior parts that the non-mages were allowed to see. The hallway and my rooms on the seventh floor looked original, but the building didn't feel old. It was clean, well-maintained, and elegant. Not musty at all.

Master Greenwood was probably one of those who built it. Dierdre looked to be about thirty, and I wondered how old she really was.

I had time to kill before dark, so I went shopping again. It wouldn't take my new employers long to figure out that I had only two outfits, and if they were paying me in addition to feeding me, I decided I could spend a few bucks.

CHAPTER 11

I hit the Tracker Lounge for dinner, expecting the place to be full of talk about the demon. I wasn't disappointed.

"Ah, hell, there ain't no such thing as demons," I heard a voice say as I passed a table while carrying my drink from the bar.

"Twelve feet tall, bright red all over, with muscles like a weightlifter on steroids," I said, stopping and facing the speaker. "What would you call it?"

"That's just bullshit. You can't believe the rumors."

I grinned. "I saw it. Saw it pick up a woman and bite her head off."

The tables around us grew quiet.

"You're the girl who took down Madeleine du Mont," a voice said from behind me.

I turned around and said, "Yes, and I've seen my share of monsters. Never seen one like that."

Several people asked questions, and I answered them as best as I could. Yes, it just disappeared after running amok for six blocks. Yes, there were people killed and more injured. Yes, the

TV stations showed up, but the cops wouldn't let them get close.

"Have you ever smelled brimstone?" I asked after a while. "It's a stink you'll never forget."

"How do you know it was brimstone?"

"That's what one of the master mages who showed up called it. I'll defer to his expertise."

"You said there were cops. Regular city cops?"

"Yeah, and forensic teams, and some people from the Queen City Architect's office. Some of those buildings were damaged pretty badly."

"Young lady's telling the truth," another voice said. It came from a tall bearded man I didn't know, although I'd seen him around. "I saw it, too. When the cops came, they kicked me out of the area. Never seen the mundanes go crazy like that. They couldn't believe their own eyes."

"There's no bounty posted," another man said.

"And there won't be," the tall man replied. "Only a mage can summon a demon. They'll keep this one close and try to handle it themselves."

I used people's focus on the tall man to make my escape over to a small table next to the wall. The waitress brought my order almost immediately.

But I'd taken only two bites when a woman pulled out the chair across from me and sat down. Late thirties or early forties was my guess, but I could feel her magic, so looks didn't mean anything. I didn't acknowledge her and took another bite of my pot pie.

"I'm Loretta Lighthorse," she finally said. "I'm a tracker."

Considering where we were sitting, she didn't need to add the last part. I took another bite and then a sip of my beer.

"I'm a friend of Morgan's," she said. "Are you trying to track the demon?"

I looked up then. She wore a wide-brimmed western hat, a

leather coat, and a black shirt with black leather pants. She looked Native American—brown skin, long, straight black hair, high cheekbones. I would guess she was almost as tall as I was, but she probably outweighed me by twenty or thirty pounds.

"No," I replied, and took another swallow of beer before returning my attention to the pie. But inside, I felt a tingle of excitement. Two people tracking the mage would make the job far easier.

Lighthorse smiled a little. "Smart girl. Tracking the mage?"

"Trying to keep my head down, eat my dinner, and stay alive."

She pushed a business card across the table. "If you want to join forces, give me a call. We both know that most of these so-called trackers couldn't find a floodlight at night. But someone with the right magic has a chance at finding a demon summoner."

She stood and walked off. She carried herself like a cat, smoothly strutting across the barroom floor. I wondered if she could be a shifter.

I left the card where it lay until after I finished eating, then pocketed it without looking at it.

My next stop was at Nick's Cellar. It was crowded, and there weren't any tables open. I did manage to snag a barstool.

At one point, I overheard a customer talking to the bartender, Jack, about the demon.

"Some say demons don't exist, some insist they do. Doesn't matter. For my money, I think we're seeing the beginning of a civil war inside the Guild."

The bartender laughed. "And how would they keep that quiet? I mean, the Guild doesn't exist only here. There are Guild Halls all over the world, and some places don't have one at all. The Guild is about as unified as the United Nations. I don't think they're organized enough to have a civil war."

After the customer took his drink back to his table, I said to the bartender, "That's not the first time I've heard about strife inside the Guild."

He nodded. "And it's best for people like you and me to keep our noses out of it. My brother is a Guild mage, and when they get nasty, they get really nasty. Ethics and morality take a backseat to raw power."

I hesitated to ask my next question, but I really wanted to know the answer.

"I thought that there were Guild families. I mean, the mages train their own. Not true?"

He shook his head. "I have some magic, but not enough for them. I can keep peace in a place like this, but the best I could do with the Guild was to be a security guard. I make more money here and don't have to follow all their stinking rules and put up with their damned arrogance."

"I think my father said something like that one time."

He smiled. "I knew your dad. Lee had plenty of magic, but the arrogance of the mages pissed him off, and he didn't want to live by all their restrictions. Your mom was Guild until she hooked up with your dad."

I hadn't known that. If they had rejected the Guild, it made more sense that the mages hadn't tried to rescue me when I was orphaned.

CHAPTER 12

I showed up at the Guild Hall the following morning and asked for Marlene. I waited for about five minutes, and a young woman showed up.

"Kaitlyn? I'm Marlene."

Her smile was infectious. She stuck out her hand for me to shake. My suitcase was in her other hand.

"Shall we dump this in your room, and then we can get you oriented. Dierdre left some lessons for you, too."

We went up to the seventh floor, and Marlene made me operate the elevator and the lock into my room.

I surveyed her while we rode up to my room. The top of Marlene's head reached my chin. She had short, dark-brown unruly hair, a round face with prominent cheekbones, and appeared to be just a little plump. The smile never left her face, and everything she did was filled with exuberant energy.

"When did they get my retinal picture?" I asked as we stood in the elevator.

"I think they took it when they tested you, didn't they?"

I remembered looking into some device, but Olinsky and the bald man hadn't told me the purpose of anything they did.

So, the Guild had my retinal patterns and handprint. That meant it would be almost impossible to hide from them if I needed to.

"This floor is for apprentices," she said. "My room is around the corner. Students are housed at the Farm. We'll have to wait for Dierdre to show you that. I don't have permission to use the portal."

Marlene took me around to the cafeteria and the dining room, and to the commissary to show me where to get any supplies I might need, such as toothpaste and soap. There was a laundry where I could take my towels and linens and exchange them for fresh. She said they would even wash my clothes for me.

The first level basement held a gym, a swimming pool, and racquetball courts. There was even a fencing pitch. The second level was a car park. I knew it was a large building—eighteen stories plus the three-level basement, and it covered a city block—but I never guessed it was a self-contained fortress, built and equipped to withstand a siege.

We ate lunch in the cafeteria on the first floor above the ground level, and the food was first-rate. I couldn't believe it was not only free but I could also take anything I wanted, and eat until I was stuffed.

After lunch, we went to a small office and sat down at a table. Marlene pulled some sheets of paper out of a folder and handed them to me.

"You need to memorize these, and practice drawing them. It's probably best at first to draw them on paper, but you'll need to learn to draw them in the air, and they have to be perfect."

The pages held runes, each with a word. Some of them I recognized, such as the rune used to cast a ward and the simplest one that I used to cast my personal shield. But others were labeled fire, wind, force, block, and vortex.

I shook my head. "I can't do anything with fire. Why should I practice it?"

"Do you know what a ley line is?" she asked.

"I've heard the term. It has something to do with arcane spells, right?"

She shook her head, her curls thrashing back and forth.

"It has everything to do with arcane spells – with mage spells. The ley lines are the source of our magic. There is a major ley line running through the city, and this building sits directly on it. To do real magic, you have to tap into the ley line."

"So, when I shield, that's not real magic?"

She smiled. "You are tapping into the ley line, you just don't know you're doing it. To cast your shield, you sketch that rune," she pointed to the paper, "and then you focus your will on the rune, and say the Word. Right? And you can do it really fast, because you've practiced it a million times, and because usually you're scared shitless and do it correctly."

I burst out laughing.

She cocked her head, with an expectant look on her face.

"Yeah, that's right," I said reluctantly.

"When you focus your will on the rune, you're drawing on the magic running in the ley line. At some point, someone taught you to do that. We're going to teach you how to draw all the magic you need."

She watched for a while as I practiced drawing the runes, then said, "I have a date, so let's get together at nine in the morning, okay?"

"Have fun."

"Do you have a boyfriend?"

I shook my head.

"I could introduce you to a couple of nice men."

I looked up from what I was doing. "You do know that I'm sixteen, right?"

Her eyes widened slightly, and her smile faded a little. "Oh. No, I didn't know that. You look older."

"Well, I'm not interested in boys, and I'm even less interested in men."

"Okay. Well, have a good evening."

I gathered up the papers and took them up to my room, then went back down to the dining room for dinner.

I was nervous walking into such an elegant setting, feeling that everyone would be watching me. But other than a few casual glances, no one seemed interested.

The waiter asked me my name and took my order. I took a chance and ordered a steak. There weren't any prices on the menu. He didn't blink, just asked if I'd like a glass of wine. I vaguely knew that red wine usually accompanied meat. I asked him for a recommendation.

After I ate—I couldn't finish it all—I went back to my room and took the first hot bath I'd had in two years.

The room seemed very warm, but there was a thermostat, and I turned it down, then snuggled into the blankets of a bed that didn't sag in the middle. I didn't know where this journey with the Guild would take me, but I decided I would enjoy the ride while I could.

CHAPTER 13

I worked on the runes with Marlene the following morning. We reached the point where I could draw five of them in the air. It shocked me that when I did, they hung there, a purplish-red. If I didn't draw them perfectly, they fell apart and disappeared, but when I got it right, they stayed for almost a minute until they faded away.

Marlene wouldn't allow me to say the Word to trigger any of those runes.

"We'll practice that at the training grounds," she said.

Dierdre showed up at about noon. After Marlene gave her a quick briefing on my progress, and I drew the five runes in the air, she said, "Let's go to lunch, and then we'll go out to the Farm and you can trigger them."

"I don't understand this ley line stuff," I told her. "Marlene says I've been using ley line magic to cast my shield and my wards, but I don't understand how. It's certainly nothing I'm doing consciously."

"You've lived your whole life here in Queen City," she said. "The ley line here is so strong that we're bathed in magical energy even if we're not aware of it. Anyone with even the slightest bit of magical affinity can do some magic without training or understanding what they're doing."

She took my hands in hers.

"Close your eyes and feel. I'm going to show you how to tap the ley line."

I didn't feel anything at first, then there was kind of a buzzing, a tingling feel on my skin. And then, like a dam bursting—I was immersed in a roaring river of energy that filled every cell in my body. An overwhelming amount of energy that made me feel like I was going to explode.

I dropped her hands, pushed myself away from her, and stood, whirling about and striding across the room. The energy was still there—I could feel it—but outside of me, instead of pouring through me. I knew that if I reached out with my mind, I could draw it into me again, and it scared the hell out of me.

"Holy shit!"

"That is what you pull on and feed into the runes when you trigger them," Dierdre said. "And if you can't control the amount of power you channel, the results can be disastrous. That's why we train students far away from the city."

I was shaking like a leaf. "I can't do that. Damn!" I spun around to face her. "That would tear me apart!" The image of Crazy Harry, the old drunk at Nick's, flashed through my mind. I suddenly understood what had happened to him.

"That happens sometimes," Dierdre said. "That's why you need to control it."

She stood. "Let's get some lunch and talk about it."

I wasn't sure I could eat. My stomach, along with the rest of me, was going nuts, doing flip-flops. But I dutifully followed them to the dining room. I was afraid the whole way that my legs would give out.

We ordered food, and Dierdre said, "Let's start with a basic lesson in the theory of magic, shall we? There are several types of magic practiced around the world. The two most common in Western countries are witch magic and mage magic. Do you know the difference?"

I shook my head.

"A witch pulls on energy from the world around her and uses some sort of ritual or spell to twist reality. Some may pull their energy from the earth or plants or animals, or even from something like an electrical line. They study and experiment and learn how to use that energy to cast their spells. Witches can use runes to focus their magic, but they don't use ley lines to trigger them. With me so far?"

"Yeah. I think so."

"Okay. There are other energy sources that run throughout the earth called ley lines, and that is where mages get their power. Depending on how far a mage is from a line, and how powerful the line is, determines how much power he or she can pull from the line and use. Think of them like rivers and streams of raw magic of varying sizes. Mages tend to have an affinity for a particular type of magic. A mage twists, or converts, ley energy into a physical manifestation. Like with fireballs and lightning bolts. We call that pyromancy and electrokinesis."

"Got it."

"There are five major arcane elements: fire, earth, air, water, and spirit. There's a rare kind of mage we call a ley line mage, who doesn't interact with any of the elements. They pull ley line energy and redirect it. They don't convert it. Think of it as a sledge hammer—very little subtlety. A ley line mage might be able to knock down a building, but can't light a candle."

"Okay." I could see that. The energy I had felt in the ley line would be almost impossible for anything to withstand.

"Then there's the rarest talent. We call them spirit mages. They are able to manipulate the energy forces that tie the world together, that confine the physical elements. Some spirit mages are called rune mages, because they do their work through using runes powered by the ley lines. But sometimes the runes aren't necessary. Some mages can focus without them."

The waiter brought our orders, and Marlene dug into hers. Dierdre was watching me closely. I stared at my BLT, which smelled wonderful, but I couldn't summon any appetite for it. My mouth was dry, so I took a drink of my coke.

"You think I'm one of those spirit mages?"

"Our testing shows that you may be. We don't know for sure, and we don't know how powerful you could be. But what you can do, with little training and using only the ambient ley line energy, is unusual."

I picked up my sandwich and took a bite. I couldn't taste it, and set it back down on the plate.

"You've probably never been in a dive bar called Nick's Cellar, have you?" I asked.

Dierdre's mouth crooked at one corner. "I know Crazy Harry Crawford. He's my cousin, and his daughter is one of my best friends."

I stared at her in shock.

"Harry pushed the limits. Just because the speedometer on my car says it will go one hundred twenty doesn't mean I should push the pedal to the floor on a twisty two-lane road up one of the canyons in the mountains. I think you've got a lot more common sense—and survival instinct—than that. I truly feel sorry for Harry, but stupidity is all too often poorly rewarded. Eat your sandwich."

CHAPTER 14

"We're going out to the Farm this afternoon?" I asked.
"Yes, why?"
"I need to make a phone call. I have an appointment I need to cancel."

I walked away from them and pulled out my phone. Scott Winfield and I met every Wednesday afternoon for weapons practice, and then I stayed at the dojo that evening for karate. Scott was the most supportive person I'd known since my parents died, and he would worry if I didn't show up.

"Scott, I won't be able to make it this afternoon or this evening," I said when he answered.

"Is everything all right?"

"Oh, yes, but I got a new job, and they want me here today. I'll work it out so that I have Wednesday's off."

"That sounds great. I can't wait to hear all about it. Does that mean you won't be taking on any freelance work?"

"Not necessarily. Why?"

"A lawyer friend contacted me. A twelve-year-old girl is missing. Her parents think she's been lured away by a man she met online."

"Give me the address and phone number, and I'll contact them when I get off this evening."

I wasn't sure he would be happy when I told him the real story. My father had not been a fan of the Guild, and as I recently learned, my mother had quit the organization when she married him. All of Scott's knowledge of the Mage Guild would have come from them since he had no magic of his own.

Dierdre took us to the third sub-basement. We took a right when we got off the elevator, and were presented with a dozen large cubicles with glass doors. She led us to one, closed the door, then fed magic into a rune permanently carved into the stone wall. The world ended.

I was completely disoriented when she opened the door. Dierdre and Marlene walked ahead of me through a concrete building and out into open plains. The mountains glistened in the sunshine in the distance behind us.

"What the hell?" I asked.

"This is the Farm," Dierdre said, "and the portal is about the only way to get here. Those buildings over there are where the students live." She then pointed to another set of larger buildings. "Those are the classrooms."

Her arm swept an arc to our left. "The training grounds are there. Any buildings on that side are expendable."

She walked in that direction and we followed.

"Where are we?" I asked.

"A little more than a hundred miles east of the city. The Guild owns about ten thousand acres out here, completely warded and illusioned. The ley line runs through the property."

I reached out, and could feel the ley line, but I didn't try to touch it. It roared past us in a multi-colored torrent. I closed my eyes, and although I could no longer see the line, I could hear it, like an orchestra warming up—there wasn't a melody, but rather many notes, some discordant.

"You don't have to open yourself to the entire line," Dierdre said. "You can just dip into it, like using a bucket or a ladle to take a bit of water from a river rather than trying to drink directly from it. Just reach out, and take a little bit of it."

I envisioned a window in my mind, and then opened it to look into the ley line. Reaching in, I grabbed a handful of that raging unreality. Magical energy flowed into me, filling me, but not stretching me. The world around me filled with multi-colored threads of energy. Some of the threads were very thin, others were like strings, or thicker like ropes, while still others were like ribbons of various widths. They rippled and undulated with no discernible pattern.

The colors of the threads in the dirt were brown and gray. Marlene glowed red, yellow, and electric blue. The trees and bushes pulsed green and yellow and brown.

If I closed my eyes, I somehow knew the threads were still there. I could hear them and smell them, feel them and taste them. The world pulsed with energy. Dierdre tasted of morning air in the mountains, of the clear taste of a mountain stream. And reaching farther, I could feel Marlene's heat. Smells emanated from the threads—cooking beefsteak, flowers, heavy perfume, and once I detected the smell of a rotting corpse. Not everything coming from the ley line was benign.

Opening my eyes, I saw that Dierdre was watching me closely.

"Do you understand?" she asked.

"No. But I can learn. I can survive this. You say there's a way to use it? To do things with this energy?"

She smiled. "Yes, you can do a great deal with it. Draw the rune for fire, and then trigger it with the Word while pushing ley line magic into it."

I faced away from her and did as she said. It produced a stream of flame about as big around and as long as my arm. Pretty pitiful, actually, but I was impressed. It didn't really involve all the threads of magic swirling about me. It did, however, involve all the colors of the ley line. All those that were connected to fire as well as those that weren't.

"Wouldn't it be easier just to grab the threads I need and direct them?" I asked.

"The threads?" Dierdre's expression was one of bafflement. "You mean the whole ley line?"

"No, the threads I pull out of it." I reached out and grabbed a bunch of the red threads and a couple of ribbons, pulled them together, and then pushed them the way I had the raw magic into the rune. A gout of flame shot out at least fifty feet in front of me, immolating the brush in its path. The plants screamed in torment, shredding my composure. I could feel their pain.

I felt a jolt, and realized my legs had given out. I sat on my butt in the dust, staring in dismay at what I had done. The echoes of the plants' demise bounced around in my head, and my nerves felt as though they were on fire.

"Great goddess," Dierdre breathed. She knelt down beside me. "Are you all right?"

I shook my head. "I don't want to do that again."

After a while, when I felt better, I tried to explain to her and Marlene what I experienced when I pulled on the ley line, but they didn't seem to understand. They told me the colors I saw around them were manifestations of their auras, but the threads and ribbons of magic I saw, heard, felt, tasted were something they had never experienced.

When I tried to tell them that when they pulled magic from the ley line, I could see them pulling the threads, they just shook their heads.

"I've never heard anyone explain magic that way," Dierdre said.

"I pull magic. Magic I can feel and use," Marlene said. "I don't know what kind of magic you or Dierdre uses."

Dierdre took us back to the city, and I went to my room. I was extremely tired for some reason, and I fell asleep.

CHAPTER 15

It was eight o'clock in the evening when I woke up, my stomach growling at me. I figured I had just enough time to catch Scott at the dojo, so I cruised through the cafeteria and grabbed a sandwich and a bottle of orange juice.

One bus transfer took me to the dojo, and I arrived just before he closed up at nine.

"Hey, the working woman," he called when he saw me come in.

I could picture Scott in either a Three Musketeers movie or as Bruce Lee's American sidekick. He was about my height, wiry and strong, with brush-cut sandy-blond hair, handsome, with a ready smile.

"I wanted to swing by and talk to you before I called the girl's parents," I said.

"Well, her name is Sarah Wilkinson. She's twelve—almost thirteen—and her parents are convinced she's been chatting with boys online. One in particular seems to be older. Their lawyer brought in a hacker, who cracked her passwords."

I nodded. "Pedophile or trafficker or both. How long has she been gone?"

"She didn't come home from school yesterday. The school also says she didn't show up yesterday."

"Well, let's hope she's still in the state," I said, reaching for my phone. I called the parents, and they told me to come by.

Scott gave me a ride over there and dropped me off. The house was in a new townhouse development that was part of the downtown gentrification.

"What's the new job?" he asked on our way to their home.

"The Mage Guild. They think I have potential. They'll give me a free place to live, free food, and pay me a stipend. They'll train me."

He shrugged. "And they still let you out at night?"

"They still want to use me as a tracker. I figure I can try it out, and if I don't want to stay, I can leave. Mom did."

"Yes, she did." The way he said that made me wonder if I knew the whole story.

I usually adopted a glamor that made me look ten years older before I went into the clients' homes. After verifying with the Wilkinsons what Scott had told me, I looked at the chat stream between Sarah and her new boyfriend. He certainly didn't use language I would expect from a boy of fourteen, and his picture—which I assumed was fake—looked more like that of a seventeen-year-old model in a teen magazine.

Sarah's bedroom reminded me of mine when I was that age. Posters of the hottest bands and singers, lots of stuffed animals. I snooped around a little and found some makeup hidden in her closet. Her mom gave me a hairbrush of Sarah's, which was all that I needed.

"I'll call sometime tomorrow and give you an update," I told them. "I may find her tomorrow, but I really wouldn't expect something that quick. Your lawyer explained my rates? And I'll provide receipts for any expenses I have."

Her father was eyeing me, obviously a little skeptical. "You have had some success at this?" he asked.

I pulled out a 3x5 card with names and phone numbers, and handed it to him. "These are clients I've worked with in the past. Your problem, unfortunately, is not unusual. I can wait while you call any of them you like."

He took me at my word—the dads were usually skeptical. He went into another room and closed the door. Twenty minutes later he was back.

"I apologize," he said, "but you know, one has to be sure."

"I understand. There are a lot of scammers in the world. Now, can someone walk me to her bus stop?"

Both of her parents went with me. But before we reached it, I stopped.

"This is as far as she got," I said. "She got in a car here."

That wasn't as much of a problem as a city bus would have been. I could track a car as easily as a person. Hopefully, her 'friend' didn't take the freeway. That *would* present a problem, especially if he drove to the other side of town. I couldn't run seventy miles an hour, and tracking Sarah twenty or thirty miles on foot would take a while.

"Thanks," I said to her parents. "That's all I needed to know." I struck out in the direction the car had taken, but I wasn't really following it. I was headed to my flat to get my bicycle.

I noted when my route diverged from that of the boyfriend's car. It didn't appear that he was going toward one of the freeways. It looked like he planned to take her to one of the less-savory fringe areas of downtown, which made sense. I had found kids who were kidnapped by mansion-dwelling pervs, but mostly the low-life scum who played the game were broke and into drugs.

The busses were on reduced schedules in the late evenings, and notoriously unreliable. By the time I'd walked most of the way home, it was past eleven, and I knew I'd never go out hunting that late. So I stopped into

Nick's, which was on the way home, to have a beer before bed.

It was a typical late evening in the bar, full of smoke, and a few people getting a little rowdy. Things rarely got out of hand as the bartender—I never did figure out if he was Nick—was big and tough enough to wrestle alligators.

I found a small table in a corner, and sat back to watch. After a while, I got curious and reached out to the ley line. Immediately, the colored threads and ribbons overlaid the room.

My eyes were drawn to Crazy Harry. Instead of the kind of aura I'd seen with Dierdre and Marlene, Harry was almost invisible inside a multi-colored sphere of chaos. The strings were pulled into him and exploded into points of light. It was evident there was no order in his presence.

But the magic-filtered vision clarified what the other people in the bar were. Some showed almost no aura at all. Others had muted auras similar to Dierdre or Marlene, and some took on the hues of the earth and plants I had seen at the Farm. The strongest aura in the place belonged to the tall, bearded man I had seen in the Tracker Lounge the night of the demon's rampage through downtown. I could pick out elements of fire as well as air surrounding him.

And then Loretta Lighthorse sat down in the chair across from me.

"How goes the demon hunting?" she asked.

"I don't know. I've been busy, but I haven't heard of any new manifestations. Have there been?"

She shook her head. "Not that I've heard."

Her aura was very different than everyone else's—gray and kind of foggy. Not clear or sharp at all. I wondered what kind of magic that reflected.

"Can I buy you a drink?" she asked. "Collected a bounty today, so feeling a bit flush."

I shrugged. "Sure. An amber ale."

She got up and walked across to the bar. Even in middle age, she had a pretty good figure. And she was pretty. But there was something about her that made me uneasy.

She came back and set a fresh mug of ale and a shot glass of brown liquid in front of me. Raising her own shot glass, she said, "Cheers!"

"Uh, I don't drink hard liquor."

"Just one. To celebrate the demise of one more vampire."

I clinked my glass on hers and swallowed the shot. It burned like crazy, but not as bad as most of the whiskey I had tried before.

"Why the bounty?" I asked, taking a sip of my beer to quench the burn.

"He was turning kids, mainly teenagers and college kids."

There were two things the Guild forbade vampires—draining their victims to death, and turning them into new vampires. And the penalty for turning underage people was the final death.

"How many?"

"The Guild thinks maybe fifteen or twenty."

I took a deep breath. "So, we'll soon have fifteen or twenty more bounties posted."

"Probably. Word is that a couple of werewolves were found drained this week."

New vamps, without a parent to guide and teach them, almost invariably went rogue. Without any self-restraint and full of blood-lust, they took too many people, killed their victims, and often left them where the human authorities would find them. Bad business all the way around. Usually, the Guild preferred to round them up and give them to one of the elder vamps to train.

And if some vamps were stupid enough to kill werewolves, it

could precipitate the kind of inter-species warfare that was being reported in Atlanta and Dallas. Fun times ahead.

CHAPTER 16

My bicycle wasn't new, and it wasn't flashy, but I had bought the ten-speed mountain bike from a student of Scott's for a hundred dollars. I checked, and the same bike new was more than five times that amount. So what if the paint was scratched and the frame had a couple of dings?

Starting at five in the morning from where I'd left off the previous evening, I followed the magical scent of the car carrying Sarah. Two hours later, I chained the bike to a stand in front of a busy coffee shop, set a ward on it, and continued on foot. I was in a run-down residential area, and assumed my prey was the tenant of one of the cheap apartments.

Three blocks later, I stood in front of a blue car—a lot older than my bike and in worse shape. I was holding Sarah's brush in my hand, and her scent was very strong. It seemed as though the ring Master Greenwood had given me enhanced some aspects of my magic. The trail led away from the car and into the front door of what had once been a fairly large home. According to the mailboxes inside the entranceway, it had been carved up into six apartments.

There were two doors off the hallway on the ground floor,

but my trail led up the stairs. On the next floor, my destination proved to be the door on the left. I continued down the hall to the window at the end. Outside was the fire escape landing. The window was painted shut, and judging from the amount of dirt caked on the sill, no one had gone in or out that way in a very long time.

I crept back down the hall to the door that hid my objective. Kicking in a door wasn't as easy as they made it look on TV. A personal shield, however, created a surface as hard as steel, and protected the mage from any damage. The door didn't look very substantial, but I had hoped to make a quieter entrance. Kicking in the door and beating the snot out of the kidnapper was the thing a father would do in such a situation. A softer approach would make it far easier to get Sarah's cooperation.

Living on the streets as long as I had, and associating with the other characters whose existence was mostly ignored by society, I had picked up a few tricks. My lock picks made quick work of the main door lock.

I adopted the glamor that added ten years to my age—the persona that was state licensed as a private investigator. Then I cast my personal shield and opened the door.

Rushing inside, I raced through the living room, past the kitchen, and found two bedrooms separated by the bathroom. I stuck my head in the room on the left and saw Sarah sitting in the middle of the bed, naked, an expression of astonishment on her face. She looked younger than she had in the pictures her parents showed me.

The naked man standing next to the bed raised a pistol and fired. The bullet ricocheted off my shield.

I didn't want any more of that. A wild bullet could hit Sarah. I rushed the man and kicked him in the shin. I was rewarded with the sound of bone cracking. I clubbed him in the head and he went down. A second blow, and his body relaxed as he dropped into unconsciousness. He was larger than me, and probably stronger, but the personal shield gave me all the advantage I needed.

"Sarah Wilkinson? Get dressed." I dropped the shield and bent to pick up the gun. The room smelled of sex. I looked the man over. He appeared to be in his late twenties.

"Who the hell are you?"

"I said get dressed. I'm taking you home."

She bitched a little more, telling me that she and 'Ron' were in love. Finally, I grabbed her by the hair and pulled her face close to mine.

"I said, get dressed. I'm calling the cops right now, and if you want to parade around nude for them, and for your parents, then go ahead."

I let go of her and pulled out my phone. I didn't call the cops, or even her parents. I called the lawyer who was going to pay me. "Mr. Baxter? This is Katy Brown. I have her, and the pervert who seduced her. I suggest you bring the police with you." I gave him the address and hung up. Then I emptied the bullets from the revolver and dropped them into my pocket so as to prevent any unfortunate accidents.

Sarah had to collect her clothes from various parts of the bedroom. What that SOB had done to her made me sick. I nudged the perv with my shoe a couple of times, and finally he began to rouse. Grabbing him by the hair, I pulled his head off the floor and pushed the barrel of the revolver against his temple.

"What's your name?" I asked. "Your real name."

His eyes shifted sideways, trying to see the gun. I pushed the barrel a little harder into his skin.

"George Pattinson."

"Very good. That better be the name on your driver's license. Where's your phone?"

His eyes shifted toward the nightstand. I let go of his hair and stood, still pointing the gun at him, then retrieved the phone. Grabbing his hand, I pushed his index fingertip against the screen, and the phone came alive.

There were pictures, of course. A number of them were of Sarah, but also of four or five other girls. None were as young as Sarah, but all were too young to drive.

Sarah was mostly dressed and inching toward the door. I pointed the pistol at Pattinson and said, "Sarah, sit down or I'll blow his head off."

She hurriedly glanced around. Other than the bed, there wasn't any place to sit.

"Sit on the floor."

She did, with gratifying speed.

I pushed the barrel against Pattinson's head again.

"Now, George, who were you planning to sell her to?"

"I don't know what you're talking about."

I cocked the pistol.

"Romero. Enrique Romero."

I thumbed through his contacts on the phone until I found Romero.

"And how do I find him?" I asked.

"He runs girls out on East Colfax."

"When he doesn't move them out of state," I said. George nodded.

I got off the floor and sat on the edge of the bed, scrolling through the pictures on his phone. They were enough to land him a prison sentence even without the kidnapping charge.

"Hello?" a man's voice called from outside the apartment.

"Mr. Baxter?"

"Yes, and I have the police with me."

"Come on in. Back bedroom."

Two uniformed cops came in, followed by a detective and the lawyer. I handed the pistol to the first cop, then fished in my pocket and handed him the bullets. Pattinson's eyes got really wide.

"He took a shot at me when I first came in, so I decided he shouldn't be allowed to play with his toy anymore."

The detective chuckled.

Baxter knelt down by Sarah. "Are you all right?"

She didn't answer him, just turned her head away.

"I'd suggest a rape kit, an STI screen, and Plan B," I said. "Her playmate doesn't seem to understand the concept of age-appropriate games."

I handed Pattinson's phone to the detective. The image on the screen said more than a thousand words.

"Ms. Brown?" he asked.

I pulled out my PI license and showed it to him.

"Can you come in this afternoon and give us a statement?" he asked.

"Not a problem."

Very shortly, the cops had Pattinson in clothes and handcuffs, and led him away. A lady cop showed up, and she and the detective put Sarah in a car to take to the hospital. A couple of forensics people came in and kicked Baxter and me out.

After he called Sarah's parents, he turned to me.

"I really didn't expect you'd find her so quickly."

"It's not my first rodeo, and the type of guys who pull this kind of crap aren't very smart."

"Well, what do I owe you?"

"Five hundred a day for two days. And breakfast. I started this morning at five o'clock, and I'm starving."

CHAPTER 17

Most of the money Baxter gave me went into the safe at Scott's dojo. That's where I did my banking. After the bank conspired with my grandparents to steal all my parents' money and their house, I had a very poor opinion of such institutions.

The bus dropped me off at the police station, and I gave the detective my statement. It wasn't the first time I'd done that, so I was pretty relaxed and confident. But he hit me with something I wasn't expecting.

"Mr. Pattinson has accused you of breaking and entering," the cop said. "His lawyer is screaming illegal search because you didn't have a search warrant."

"The door was open, and I heard the girl, so I went in to protect her. I didn't know she was being sexually assaulted, but when I saw that, I think I was within my rights to interrupt a crime in progress, don't you? Then the bastard tried to shoot me, so I disarmed him."

The detective offered the hint of a smile and said, "Stick with that story. Black belt?"

I shrugged. "Purple, ready to test for brown. I was following a man who kidnapped a young girl. Am I supposed to just go away because he shut a door? Call you and wait for a warrant? Tell me what to do next time."

He shook his head, but didn't answer, and sent me away.

Out of curiosity the following day, I checked the bounty board at the Guild Hall before going past the security desk. Nothing new was posted. Nothing about mages who were summoning demons. But under the 'paid' list there was a vampire accused of turning adolescents. That reminded me of Loretta Lighthorse's aura.

I found Marlene in her office.

"There you are," she said. "Dierdre was asking about you."

"I had some business I had to take care of."

"Well, you have some business here you have to take care of, too." She sounded a little irked.

"Perhaps if you gave me a schedule or something," I said.

"Come on. Let's go find Dierdre."

As we walked down the hall, she said, "Students usually don't go anywhere."

"Students usually aren't told by masters to hunt down demon summoners."

She shot me a glance, but didn't continue the conversation.

Dierdre was in her office, and I wondered again what she did when she wasn't babysitting me. And was it standard for an air mage to have a fire mage for an apprentice? In many ways, she and Marlene struck me as complete opposites.

"So, have you practiced your runes or done anything with ley lines since the last time I saw you?" Dierdre asked.

"I've been looking at people's auras."

"Anything interesting? Do you think you understand what you're seeing?"

"To a certain extent. People who have magic have significantly more evident auras than people who don't, and you can use that to tell who the mages are, and what their magic is."

"People's auras can change," she said, "depending on their moods, their physical and mental health. And sometimes one aspect of their magic may be more prominent than at other times."

That made sense.

"But there was one woman whose aura completely baffled me. The color—only a single color—was a foggy gray."

Dierdre cocked her head to the side, and a line deepened between her brows. "I don't think I've ever seen one like that. Have you tried using your talent on a vampire?"

I shook my head. "They don't tend to hang out in tracker bars."

She laughed. "When I look at a vampire, the aura is black. They really aren't alive in the usual sense, although they aren't dead, either. Shifters usually have a brown core to their aura, which is larger and brighter in their animal form than in their human form. The viruses don't just change their human bodies, but their minds and personalities as well."

"I had wondered—before you showed me how to connect to the ley line—if she was a shifter of some kind. But she doesn't feel like a wolf shifter. Are there other kinds?"

"There are some cat shifters, but none native to North America. By that, I mean no werepumas. But there are jaguar shifters in Central and South America. And I've heard of weretigers in Asia, but I've never met anyone who has seen one."

"Would that be a different virus than the one that turns people into werewolves?"

Dierdre shook her head. "I don't know. I've never studied that. But you're free to research it, in your spare time. And then there's the legend of the pricolici. They're supposedly werewolves who are turned by a vampire."

She took me out to the Farm, and had me show her the runes that I'd learned and trigger them. Then she gave me five more to learn. I was sure they were good to know—the one I used to shield myself and the one to ward my apartment were definitely useful. But it was easier to grab the ley threads directly to create the same effect as some of them.

We ate in the formal dining room that evening, and to my surprise, there was a hamburger on the menu. I ordered it, and it was the best one I'd ever eaten.

"Have there been any more demon sightings?" I asked at the end of our meal.

"Not that we've heard of," Dierdre said. "Thankfully. We're still dealing with the mess downtown. There really aren't any rational explanations, and the damage was so extensive that some of the mundane authorities have started a formal investigation. That sort of thing tends to get out of hand."

I debated on whether to spend the night at the Guild Hall or at my apartment. The Guild was warm, and the bed was far superior, but it still seemed foreign. I had trouble going to sleep there, and had weird dreams. I wondered if there were some ways to use magic to block those out.

In the end, I decided to sleep where I was most comfortable and left the Guild Hall. A bus took me to an area in Capitol Hill I used to hang out at, near Two Fools' Tavern. The street kids congregated there, in part because of a lack of police presence at night, and partly for safety in numbers. I guess I was hoping to run into Jodi, but it was a cold night, and she had told me she didn't spend much time on the streets anymore.

There were a few kids hanging out at street level, but the majority of them had climbed to the roof of an abandoned warehouse. A bunch of kids had a fire going in an old oil drum and were passing some joints and cheap wine around. I knew a few of them, and recognized a few more. It was a fluid population.

I settled down next to a guy I knew—about my age—took a

hit from the joint he passed me, and passed it on to the girl on my other side.

"Long time," he said.

"Yeah."

"Heard you were doing some kind of Robin Hood vigilante thing."

"I'm good at finding things. Sometimes people pay me to find their kids. I'm not a fan of grownups hurting kids."

He nodded. "Sometimes ya gotta do things you don't want to. Better than being beaten by my old man."

"Grown man has no business with a twelve-year-old girl," I said.

"Truth. We haven't had too much problem with that around here lately."

"What kind of problems have you had?"

"Vamps. Sometimes they get careless, but even at the best of times, I have a problem getting enough to eat. Don't need the bloodsuckers running me down." He pulled his hand out of his coat pocket to show me a wooden stake. "They leave me alone, but some of the little ones can't defend themselves. Cowards picking on kids."

He motioned to two girls in a corner hunched over what looked like a pile of rags. I stood and walked over there. Nestled into the rag pile was a barely pubescent girl who was as pale as milk. One of her forearms was heavily bandaged.

"When?" I asked.

One of the girls looking after her said, "Last night. She ain't come to, yet. I'm afraid she won't make it."

"Where?"

"Cheesman Park. It really wasn't that long after dark."

"Come here," I said, walking away from the group and the fire, into darkness. I stopped and knelt down so my face was level with hers. "You don't tell nobody. Nobody, you hear?" I pressed a handful of bills into her hand. "You and your other friend eat, too, but anyone mess with you, tell them Katy Brown will gut them. Now, go to the drugstore and get iron pills, and then to that deli on fourteenth street—you know the one that I mean?—and buy a couple of pounds of their bloody roast beef. Buy some beef broth and orange juice, and start her on that. You've got to build her blood back, or she'll die. Understand me? She needs liquids and iron."

She stared at me, her eyes wide, and nodded.

"Her name's Caro. Carolyn. I'm Simone, and that's Lisa."

"And all of you, stay the hell away from the vamps. Find some old broomsticks or something and make some stakes. Okay?"

She nodded so hard I thought her neck might snap.

"Now, off with you, and don't say a word to anyone. No one else's business."

She turned and ran back to where her friends were. And I wondered all the way home if I had done any good or just was trying to ease my conscience.

CHAPTER 18

My dreams at the apartment that night weren't very comforting, and I woke up mad as hell at the vampire who chewed on that young girl.

I spent the early morning practicing the runes Dierdre had given me. Once I got used to drawing them, it seemed the next set got easier. Then I went down to the Guild Hall, and Dierdre and Marlene took me out to the Farm again.

"How many magical runes are there?" I asked.

"Forty-three. Then you can start combining them, and I'm not sure how many combinations work. Some don't work at all. Some spells require the combination of up to five runes, and then there are the spells that comprise a combination with a follow-on combination, et cetera. If you really want to study rune magic, you can apprentice with a rune mage. Some of them have been studying runes and their combinations and permutations for hundreds of years. I'm just trying to give you the basics."

I knew mages lived a long time, but that was a revelation. Not that I wanted to spend my life studying runes. That sounded about as interesting as becoming an accountant.

What I really wanted to know was what all the ley lines did —the threads, strings, ropes, and ribbons. 'Red equals fire' was pretty simple, and from Dierdre's aura it was easy to project that white was air and blue was water. But I didn't even have names for some of the colors I saw. I could taste and smell those colors, but that didn't necessarily give me a clue as to what part of the world they connected to.

And Dierdre was no help, since she didn't see the magic the way I did. She saw the ley line as a river with shades of white and blue.

"Are you saying that no one else sees the magic the way I do?" I asked.

"Oh, no. I'm just saying that I never heard them described that way."

That really wasn't helpful. I decided to switch topics.

"That woman I told you about, the one with the weird aura. Can mages be infected with the werewolf virus?"

From the look she gave me, the question startled her. "You've been hunting lycans, fighting them, and killing them, and don't know if you can be infected?"

"I'm shielded." Some trackers wore armor that wouldn't have been out of place in the twelfth century—boiled leather or heavy leather with chain mail. Almost all wore heavy leather gauntlets and leather clothes.

"Oh. Right."

I waited.

"Yes, I suppose we can. Of course, if you were bitten, and got to a healer quickly enough, they could cleanse your blood. And even with humans, not everyone who is bitten develops the disease."

"What about vamps? Can a mage be turned?"

She took a deep breath. "That is complicated. One, vampires tend to avoid us—at least as food. Our blood is like a drug to them, and can be addictive. A vampire who drinks from mages regularly seems to go mad, and eventually waste away and die. But yes, there have been cases of a mage being turned. It seems to do strange things to their magic, though. I don't think you have anything to worry about."

"Oh, no, that would never happen. I don't sleep with vamps, and that's the only way one could get that close to me."

Dierdre chuckled. "Your attitude mirrors mine."

"One more question. Why would a young werewolf attack a human?"

"Food. We're considered prey, but older, more experienced shifters know better than to eat people. That's one of the reasons for Guild bounties. But newly turned shifters, especially if they aren't adopted by a pack, don't know any better. Their wolf half can take control, and they make bad decisions."

"Trackers tell tales of werewolves attacking them as a way of committing suicide."

She raised an eyebrow, then nodded. "That would make some sense. I think most people are abhorred by the idea of becoming a monster. I know the idea makes me very uneasy."

※

After dinner, I went to my apartment and dressed in my grubbiest clothes. Then I took the bus to the Cheesman Park area, near the Botanical Gardens. I knew that some of the street kids hung out around there, panhandling from the tourists and others who came to see the gardens. The sun was setting as I got off the bus.

The conservatory and the greenhouses were closed, but there were still a couple of people wandering around in the outside gardens. There wasn't much to see at that time of year. The roses and other bushes had just been pruned, and I knew it would be a month or more before most of the plants started to bloom.

It was a clear night, and cold. In some ways, it was a relief from the rain and occasional snow showers we'd recently had. I approached the few people I saw, just commenting on the gardens. But to an observer too far away to hear us, it might have looked as though I was panhandling.

As darkness fell fully, I struck off toward the other side of the park, in the direction of the homeless kids' camp. The smarter idea would have been to take York to Colfax, walking in plenty of light with people around. But I was sure the girl who had been attacked had made the choice of a shorter walk in lieu of a safer one.

Most of the park was lawn, but there were some trees on the western side. That was where the vampire ambushed me.

He rushed me, and in spite of my shield, knocked me down. Then he discovered that he couldn't actually touch me, and maybe he could sense my mage blood. In any case, he pushed himself upright and started to run. I caught him across the back of one knee with my sword, and he went down.

Leaping to my feet, I reached him in two strides and brought the sword down on his other leg. He screamed and tried to stand. I cleaved his skull in half with a two-handed overhead strike.

That disabled but didn't kill him. I kicked him in the chest, then stood over him, and swung the sword down on his neck. It took another chop to completely sever the head, and I kicked it under a nearby bush.

If I had been pursuing a bounty, I would gather the head, put it in a special bag, and call the Guild to come clean up the body. I wasn't sure what the reaction would be if I told them I killed a vampire because I suspected he was targeting children. Even self-defense might not be a good enough reason for killing him without sanction.

So, as I had done with the werewolf, I left the body and headed for home.

CHAPTER 19

I stopped by the homeless kids' camp, and found the girls I had met the previous night. The wounded girl was awake, although still pale and weak.

"We did what you said," the girl I'd given the money to told me. "We been giving her the iron pills, and the orange juice seemed to pick her up. Now she's drinking the beef broth."

"Well, don't any of you go hanging out in the parks after dark. Ya hear me? I took care of that vamp, but you can't be careless."

"He's gone?"

"Gone for good."

"I still got some of the money. You want it back?"

I shook my head. "She's not going to get better overnight. You kids stay off the streets for a while, okay?"

Other than panhandling, the only way girls that age could make any money was shoplifting or turning tricks. Some ended up with a pimp. It turned my stomach, but there wasn't anything I could do about it. When they got a little older, it still was hard for them to get a job, even flipping burgers, without an address and decent clothes. In reality, the best they could do was hook up with an older person who would protect them. Like Jodi did.

※

I spent the rest of the week working with Marlene, and occasionally with Dierdre. After a while, I started to wonder if Marlene resented me. She didn't say anything directly, but I got the impression that the time Dierdre spent with me was time that Marlene used to get.

I practiced runes until I was sick of them. Since I was obviously stuck with that task until I mastered them all, I worked at it diligently. I had always been good at drawing, and had done a little calligraphy when Mom was still alive. I put those skills to work, and soon I had twenty-five runes I could sketch perfectly.

One day I talked Marlene into going out to the Sunrise Café for lunch. The cafeteria and dining room in the Guild Hall served wonderful food, but the French fries at the Sunrise were special.

It was a bright sunny day, with a warm breeze from the south. Trees were starting to bud, and some crocuses were blooming around them in planters scattered around Carlisle Square.

The disruption hit with little notice. There was a rumble that got louder, like standing next to a railroad track with an approaching train. Then the ground rippled, tilted, and a full-throated roar drowned out everything else. Cracks appeared in the pavement, and I was thrown off my feet.

I reached out to the ley line as I shielded. The threads and ribbons of magic rippled in time with the ground I lay on. But the threads I associated with the Earth were throwing a tantrum. I reached out and grabbed the ones nearest to me, trying to hold them steady. The larger ribbons were contorting, and I tried to sooth them, stroking them to unknot them.

While I was doing that, a part of my mind was saying, *What the hell? How am I doing that? How do I know how to do that?* But it came naturally, and not through any conscious volition.

A cornice on one of the older buildings fell to the street, smashing to bits and leaving a small crater in the sidewalk. A large crack appeared in another building. Windows were shattering in buildings all around the square, and more cracks appeared in the pavement.

It seemed to go on forever, with the crashing roar of the earth colliding with something else. Gradually, it subsided, and after a couple of minutes of delayed crashing of pieces of buildings falling off, an eerie silence followed.

I crawled to my feet and looked around. Marlene lay in a fetal position a few feet from me. The middle of the square was bisected by a huge crack leading to the front of the Guild Hall. It was wider than I was tall, and I couldn't see how deep it was.

"Earthquake," Marlene said, unfolding and sitting up.

"Queen City doesn't have earthquakes," I said. "At least, not like this."

"Not like this, but Colorado has quakes every so often." She sounded very matter-of-fact.

"How can you be so calm about it?" I asked. "What if we fell in that crevice over there?"

"We didn't. I grew up in California. This was a big one, though."

The only building in sight that wasn't damaged was the Guild Hall. People were starting to stream out of the other buildings, and one glance at the Sunrise Café told me we wouldn't be eating lunch there. The roof had collapsed, and people were starting to try and work their way through the debris to find people trapped inside.

Marlene reached out and grabbed my arm. "Let's get inside where it's safe. There could be aftershocks."

That huge canyon in the middle of the square ended at the

first front step of the Guild Hall. I looked at Marlene walking next to me.

She grinned and said, "Magic. Of all the places in the world with good wards, wouldn't you expect them here?"

The scene inside the Guild Hall reminded me of a disturbed anthill, but not a thing was damaged or even out of place. I walked over to the security guard.

"Did you feel the quake in here?"

He shook his head. "A bit of rolling, but otherwise, nothing. I stood by the door and watched outside. Are you all right?"

I nodded. "Yeah, I'm fine. A little shook up."

We went to Dierdre's office, but she wasn't there.

"I guess we should go to my office," Marlene said. "If she wants to find us, that would be the first place she'll look."

We didn't make it that far. Master Greenwood intercepted us in the hall.

"Were you inside or out?" he asked.

"Outside," Marlene said. "We shielded."

He nodded. "Come with me."

As we walked, he said, "That wasn't a natural earthquake."

"An earth mage," I said.

He shot me a look. "Yes. And like the demon summonings, aimed at the Guild."

We followed him onto an elevator that took us to the twelfth floor. The room he led us to was large and had three huge TV screens hanging on the walls. A news reporter was talking about the quake and the damage it caused. The camera scanned a number of different places, ending with Carlisle Square.

I heard the guy on TV say, "Very preliminary estimates place the damage at more than one hundred million dollars."

"That will get the insurance companies' attention," Marlene muttered.

I wondered how the mages were going to spin the whole

thing. Didn't scientists have ways of knowing an earthquake was going to happen?

Dierdre was standing off to the side, talking with a group of people who were watching the screen. Her father wandered over and spoke to her. She shot a glance in our direction, then they both came back to where Marlene and I stood.

"You were outside when the quake hit?" Dierdre asked.

We both dutifully nodded.

"Where?"

"On the square," Marlene said. "We were going over to Sunrise."

Dierdre immediately turned her attention to me. "What did you see?"

I let my eyes flick toward the Master, and saw that he was watching me as intently as she was.

"The threads went crazy. Not all of them, but the brown and gray ones—the ones I associate with the ground. They were rippling and jerking and bunching up. I'm not sure I can explain it."

"Did you do anything?" Master Greenwood asked in a quiet voice.

"Uh, I dunno. I, I tried to smooth them out. I'm not even sure how I did that. Or why."

He glanced at his daughter. "That was the outside interference."

"I didn't mean to! I mean, at the time, I couldn't figure out what was going on, and, well, I didn't hurt anything, did I?"

The Master shook his head. "No, you didn't hurt anything. But our geomancers were very confused. Someone was using earth magic to disturb the balance and cause the quake, and someone was trying to restore the balance, but not with earth magic."

"Then what kind of magic was she using?" Marlene blurted.

"Ah, that is the question, isn't it?" the Master replied.

CHAPTER 20

"You told me it was aimed at the Guild," I said that evening as the four of us sat down to dinner. "Surely, whoever did it knew the wards here were strong."

"There is a faction who wants to change the Guild," Master Greenwood said. "They don't like the way the Guild operates, or our relationship with the mundane world."

I shook my head. "I've heard speculation about a Guild civil war. But that doesn't make a lot of sense. And the demon summonings and this earthquake... I mean, what's the point? They hurt mundanes, but how does that strike at the Guild?"

"What do you think about those incidents?" Dierdre asked me.

"They're like terrorist attacks, but terrorists have an objective. They always want the world to know why they cut off peoples' heads. They want something. But we just have silence after the events. The other thing they remind me of is teenage vandalism. You know, bust things up for the sheer hell of it. Break windows, tag walls with spray paint, deface a statue. No reason, just nothing better to do and a lack of brains and creativity."

"Terrorists are usually organized," Marlene said.

"And vandals aren't," I replied. "Otherwise, both share common elements."

"Very interesting observations," Master Greenwood said. "Miss Dunne, I am a bit surprised at the depth of your analysis."

I felt myself blush. "I read a lot. The library is free, and they have newspapers from all over the world. It's also warm."

He nodded. Dierdre cocked her head, as she sometimes did, and Marlene gave me a bit of a side-eye. I took the opportunity to change the subject.

"Why would someone's aura be a foggy gray?" I asked the Master.

His eyebrows rose, and he cocked his head almost like his daughter did.

"And where did you see someone like that?"

"In a tracker bar."

Greenwood pursed his lips, then said, "That makes some sense. I think you've met a dhampir. A child born to a human woman impregnated by a newly turned vampire, before his sperm dies. Some call them daywalkers. Is this person a tracker?"

"I guess so. She said she collected a bounty for a vamp who was turning kids. She wanted to team up with me to find the summoner."

He gave me a bit of a smile. "Interesting."

Our meal came, and the conversation turned back to the earthquake.

We were halfway through our meal when Master Olinsky strode into the dining room. She didn't look happy. Grabbing a chair, she pulled it up to our table and sat down.

"What have you got for me?" she asked, looking at Master Greenwood.

"Good evening, Diana," Greenwood said. "So nice of you to drop in. Have you eaten?"

There was a twinkle in his eyes, but Olinsky just scowled at him.

"No. I've been with the Mayor. He's decidedly unhappy, and scared shitless. I can't say that I blame him."

"Well, I don't think I can tell you any more than you already know," Greenwood said. "We know what happened, but we don't know who or why, although Kaitlyn has a couple of theories."

He prompted me, and I explained my reasoning.

"That makes a lot of sense," Olinsky said when I finished. "You're right, no published manifesto, no demands. No one taking credit. But on the other hand, I can't see teenagers knowledgeable enough, or strong enough, to call and control a demon. Or to set off an earthquake of that size in a normally geographically stable area."

I didn't say anything. I was old enough to know that some so-called adults never grew up, they just grew older. The reason teenagers acted out was usually either from frustration or boredom—two things that might occur at any age.

"But if that is causing the incidents," I said, "then don't you have at least two mages involved? From what Master Greenwood gave me to read, I wouldn't expect the summoner also to cause the earthquake."

Olinsky shook her head. "Anyone with enough power could learn to summon a demon. It's a matter of ritual. Rune magic on steroids, if you wish. There have been students—people in their teens—who called demons. Of course, calling one and controlling one are different things. All of the young, stupid summoners I ever heard of died almost immediately. We stress that in our training."

She looked straight at me.

"I've seen one," I said. "No need to convince me."

It was the first time I saw her since Dierdre taught me to access the ley lines. Diana Olinsky's aura was white and red. Air and fire, a potent combination, and her aura that evening was sparking and spitting like a campfire.

"Is there any way you could track the mage who caused this?" she asked.

"If you can show me where he or she was standing when the spell was cast. I doubt seriously if the caster was standing in Carlisle Square. Too damned dangerous. I was there when it hit, and even shielded, I was worried I might fall into one of those cracks and get covered up. I don't do well without oxygen."

She shrugged. "Yeah, sort of my thinking as well."

※

The tornado was rather anticlimactic. The Front Range of Colorado was subject to some incredibly strong winds at times, and it wouldn't take much of an aeromancer to twist a one-hundred-mile-per-hour wind into a tornado.

It hit two days after the earthquake, starting just south of Highway Six and moving northeast toward the stadiums west of downtown. It broke apart when it hit the football stadium.

I didn't see it. When Chinook winds of a hundred miles per hour were blowing cars off the road, I usually found someplace safe and waited them out. But Dierdre hauled me out of my room afterward and dragged me down to the site of destruction.

"What do you think?" she asked me when we got out of the car just south of Mustang Stadium.

"Mine's bigger than yours."

"What?"

"Someone's playing games. I think you have some mages involved in a contest. Maybe they're betting on it. Who can cause the most damage? Get the most airtime on TV? Piss off the Mayor and Master Olinsky the most?"

She stared at the hundred-yard-wide path of rubble and turned back to me.

"You're kidding, right?"

"Occam's Razor. But I'm willing to be proven wrong. Actually, I'm considering taking a vacation to someplace like Laramie, Wyoming, until you figure it out. I'm not sure Queen City is safe. Rogue vamps and werewolves are one thing, playing God with the elements is something else. I mean, what if my personal shield isn't strong enough to withstand what a strong mage tosses out?"

"You didn't even finish high school. What's this bit with Occam's Razor?"

"I learn a lot from older people trying to impress me with how smart they are. Is this sort of thing happening in other cities? You know, major natural disasters, demons running through the streets, that sort of thing."

She shook her head. "Not that I'm aware of. This really isn't tornado or hurricane season, and I haven't heard of any earthquakes. And Father hasn't told me about any demon manifestations elsewhere."

"If this was a plot against the Guild, don't you think it would be more widespread?" I gestured toward the tornado's path. "How many dead?"

"Seventeen, with another two hundred people injured."

"I'll bet the Mayor's pissed."

"I'm not sure we've told him it was magically caused."

CHAPTER 21

More incidents that could fit either of my theories started happening. Or maybe they fit the theories simply because I was looking closer at things.

I went to the library one afternoon and took a deep dive into the news across the country. As far as I could tell, there wasn't a pattern of disasters that might be attributed to magic —except in Queen City. News concerning the Guild was almost nonexistent, as one would expect. Anyone with half a brain and an ounce of consciousness knew magic and the Guild existed, but unless demons rampaged through town, it rarely rose to a point of awareness. It was like air, taken for granted and not thought about.

But in Queen City, there were minor local disturbances that could—or could not—be attributed to magic. Nothing as attention-grabbing as a tornado or an earthquake but what could be considered as lesser attempts at those things.

The one that did catch people's attention was a Chinook wind one night that set records. More than two hundred miles an hour, the wind tore roofs from houses and businesses, rolled cars and especially trucks from the freeways, and left debris scattered all over town. And more than a few people noticed that the Guild Hall remained the one undamaged structure on Carlisle Square. Neither the earthquake nor the winds of unprecedented force touched the building.

"The Council decided your theory was incorrect," Dierdre told me one morning when I showed up at her office.

"Decided? What theory?" I had no idea what she was talking about.

"That individual mages are having a destruction contest. They've voted instead to investigate a seditious conspiracy."

"On what evidence?"

She shook her head. "This place is sort of like a church in some ways. You don't need evidence, just belief."

"Oh. So, what does that mean?"

"They have appointed an investigative committee with extraordinary authority. They can look at and into everything, interview anyone they want, and hold anyone for an indefinite period of time."

"In other words, I should go hang out in Laramie until it all blows over."

"I don't think you have anything to worry about. In the Council's estimation, no one below my level has the power to cause the events we've seen."

"And on the other hand, if they're looking for a scapegoat, I'm an easy target. None of this happened until I showed up. And if they haul out the rack and other torture devices, they could coerce me into implicating you and your father. You know that, historically, such 'committees' found the culprits even when they didn't exist. What you're saying is, they are going to conduct a witch hunt. I think Laramie sounds safer."

"I would say you're too young to be that cynical, but I guess with what you've been through that would be insulting."

"Dierdre, every so often, the cops decide to clean up the streets. Usually after a newspaper story about a mugging or a business owner complaining about the homeless people hanging around and hurting business. The pimps and hookers take a vacation, while all the homeless—the true street people—get rousted. Their squats are destroyed, a lot of them are arrested on one pretense or another, and all the street kids they catch end up in the Social Services system. And a month later, everything and everybody returns to normal. I'm telling you, Laramie."

"Out of curiosity, why Laramie and not Cheyenne or Colorado Springs?"

"Because Cheyenne and C Springs are where the pimps and hookers and drug dealers go. Laramie is a college town. I'm safer there."

She dropped the subject, and we went out to the Farm for my magic lesson. I had settled into a routine of executing the rune magic she wanted me to learn, but I also practiced using the threads of power I could draw from the ley line. I was astonished at the difference in the two methods.

When I returned to my room in the Hall after our lesson, I found a man waiting for me.

"Kaitlyn Dunne?"

"Yes?"

"Why do you have a ward set on your room?"

"To keep people out. Why do people normally set wards?"

"I need to search your room."

"Ah. And why is that?"

"Council authorization. All rooms on this floor need to be examined."

"Why?"

He didn't handle the five-year-old's 'why' game as gracefully as my mother had. He attempted to grab my arm. Call me paranoid, but I had shielded as soon as I saw him leaning on the wall across from my door.

"Unless you can show me your authorization, and answer

why you need to search my room, I think we're at a stalemate," I said. I turned and walked back to the elevator, reaching for my phone to call Dierdre. As the elevator doors opened, I looked back and saw the guy in the hall pulling out his phone.

Dierdre answered, and I said, "It's Kaitlyn. There's a guy who says he wants to search my room, but he won't tell me who he is or why he wants to search it. Gave me some grief because of the ward."

"Oh, dear. Where are you now?"

"Leaving."

"Wait for me in the dining room. I'll come down and we'll sort things out."

I didn't want to wait for an hour while she drove from her house—wherever that might be.

"Don't do that. I'll come by your office in the morning."

I left the Hall and started across the square to the bus stop. I noticed a man going in the same direction but didn't pay him much attention. He got on the bus with me. Tall, dark hair, wearing jeans and a hoodie.

But when he transferred to the same bus that I did, I made a point of memorizing his face. The confrontation with the man outside my room had me a little unsettled, and the possibility of someone following me home made me frantic. I rode through three stops, and got off on the fourth. He got off with me.

It was just the two of us at a bus stop without any stores or houses near, and it was getting dark. I wandered away, then leaped to the chain-link fence behind the stop. Scrambling to the top, I threw myself over and jumped to the ground. As I ran away, I looked over my shoulder and saw him climbing the fence.

I hadn't picked that spot at random. The freeway ran about fifty or sixty yards away, and in its shadow was a homeless camp.

Not one that the street kids would use, but adults, most of whom were pretty rough. A lot of alcohol and hard drugs.

But I had one friend who had squatted there for as long as I'd been on the streets. One-eyed Jack was a tracker, and a damned good one, before the heroin took over his life. If he was there—and conscious—then I'd have an ally.

I wove my way between the pitiful blanket tents and cardboard cabins, grateful of my shield. A couple of men tried to grab me but just slid off.

Jack was 'home,' to my relief. He shacked up with another addict known as Lullaby Lou, because she had a habit of humming when she was high.

"Jack! Hey, Jack. You in there?" I called from outside his squat. I knew better than stick my head in uninvited. He had some strange magic, and I wasn't sure my shield would give me complete protection from it.

"Who's there?" His raspy voice didn't have the drugged slur I would expect if he was nodding.

"It's Katy Brown. Jack, I got a problem. There's a narc following me."

He practically exploded through the blanket that served as a door for his lean-to.

"Where?"

I pointed back the way I came. "Someone told him that I knew who was supplying this camp, and he wants to take me in and sweat me. He's wearing a gray hoodie."

"Oh, yeah? What business is it of his?"

Jack rousted out several other men and a couple of women camped nearby, and started back toward the bus stop. I didn't stick around, but cast a glamor of invisibility, climbed the fence behind Jack's squat, and dropped down onto the freeway. A hundred yards away, I took the off-ramp, scampered under the freeway, and came out at another bus stop.

I knew every bus route and their schedules in the main part

of Queen City. It was a game Jodi and I used to play. She never lost. But the knowledge had value for a tracker who didn't own a car. I took the next bus, rode two stops, and transferred to a bus that took me two blocks from home.

The last time I'd been to my apartment was before the earthquake. The rickety stairs leading up to the third floor still stood, but they were shakier than ever. I took the time to cast a ward to stabilize them, as well as block anyone from using them. I hadn't seen any more followers, but a good tracker might show up later. After that, I climbed the stairs, let myself into my flat, and spent the night there.

CHAPTER 22

Dierdre was at her desk when I showed up the following morning. She motioned me to a chair and continued typing on her computer. After a couple of minutes, she looked up and pushed the computer aside.

"So, I told you they were going to be searching everyone and everything."

"Only my room? There was just one guy, no one else was around, and he was waiting for me. I might be paranoid, but the Queen City cops are notorious for planting evidence and roughing up suspects. I want some witnesses when they come at me."

"Just because you're paranoid doesn't mean no one's out to get you," Master Greenwood's voice sounded behind me.

I had heard someone come in, but hadn't known who it was. I turned toward him. "Exactly. And after I left the Hall, someone followed me. Not the same guy."

"Were you anywhere near the mousetrap?" he asked, catching me off guard. That was the common name for the convoluted interchange of two interstate highways and a couple of other major freeways north of downtown.

"Why? Yes, I passed by there, trying to shake him."

"Security reports that three of our people were attacked there. A mini riot at a homeless camp was how it was reported to the city police."

I shrugged. "I know the camp you're talking about, and the city cops leave it alone. Not a safe place."

He gave me a hard look, but I met his eyes, and he dropped the issue.

"Dierdre," he said, "call David Simpson and have him meet you at Kaitlyn's room. Supervise his search. Is that acceptable, Kaitlyn?"

"Yes, sir. I don't mean to be a pain—"

He held up a hand to cut me off. "I brought you here, and if I had any doubts, you wouldn't be here. But I need the rest of the Council to look in other directions, so let's get this behind us."

"There isn't anything in your room you wouldn't want someone to find, is there?" Dierdre asked me.

I shook my head. "Clothes, a toothbrush."

The Master left, and Dierdre picked up the phone. After a brief conversation with whoever was on the other end, she hung up, stood up, and motioned me to follow her.

A ruggedly handsome man with gray at his temples met us at my room. He was wearing the same clothes as the men from the previous evening, and I realized it was some sort of uniform. I dissolved the ward and used my handprint to let him in. Dierdre followed him, and I waited in the hall.

They were in there for about fifteen minutes. It shouldn't have taken that long. Other than a few items of clothes, the drawers and the closet were empty. I guess they had to check for false bottoms and stuff like that. Hell, I could have glamored a rocket launcher and stashed it behind the bathroom door. But since I hadn't, they came out empty-handed.

"Thank you for your cooperation," the man I took for David Simpson said. "It's a stressful time for all of us."

"Is that the uniform for Guild security?" I asked Dierdre as Simpson walked away.

"Yes. David is the director of the security service, and a good friend of mine and a supporter of Dad's. He's a straight shooter. Don't be afraid to ask him for help if you need it."

⁂

That evening, I stopped by the homeless camp the street kids had staked out on the rooftop. I found the girl who had been attacked by the vampire, and one of her friends.

"How's the arm?"

"Pretty much healed up. Still weak, and I don't know if it will ever work properly," she said, pulling up her sleeve to show me the scars. "Thank you. Simone and Lisa told me what you did. Probably saved my life."

"Just be smarter," I said. "You can't count on luck." I looked around. "Where's the other girl? The blonde?"

The older of the three girls wasn't anywhere in sight.

"Simone?" She shook her head. "Haven't seen her for two days. Some guy offered her a hundred dollars to go with him."

I pumped her for as much information as I could get. Simone Dial, age fifteen, from somewhere around Castle Rock. In my PI persona, I could check with the cops and find out if they had any information on her. But I had a bad feeling.

Just on the off chance, I took a bus east on Colfax, looking at the girls on the street. Usually, the pimps didn't put the really young ones out in public. Just advertised them by word of mouth. Simone didn't show up on the bus ride either up or back. I took a transfer and went to the Tracker Lounge for a beer before going home to sleep.

I was about halfway through my beer when my phone rang. It was Dierdre.

"Where are you?" she asked as soon as I answered.

"At the Tracker Lounge."

"Thank God. Stay there. I'll come and get you."

Okay.

She showed up about twenty minutes later. Walked in, looked around, and strode to my table once she located me. Every eye in the place was on her. Women like Dierdre didn't frequent the Tracker.

She leaned close and said, "The demon is out again. Just rampaged through that homeless camp of yours. Destroyed damned near everything and set the rest on fire. Let's go."

I looked down at my half-finished beer, wondering if I needed the alcohol or would just throw it up once I saw the demon's work. I decided to leave it be and rose to follow her.

"The same demon?" I asked as I settled into the car seat.

She handed me her phone. "That video was taken by someone who saw it and posted it on the internet."

I played the vid, and it sure looked like exactly the same demon. I handed her phone back as she pulled out of the parking lot.

"We assume there's only one summoner, and he's calling the same demon every time," she said. "You have to have the demon's name, so it's not like the summoner would have a menu to choose from. As you can see, it's a fire demon, which we suspected from the scorch marks on the buildings downtown."

She drove from downtown out toward the interchange, staying on the surface street paralleling the freeway. As we approached the scene, the sky lit up with the flashing lights of dozens of emergency vehicles—cops, firetrucks, and ambulances.

Dierdre pulled over and stopped. We were a hundred yards from the camp, but close enough to see the destruction. The chain-link fence around the area at the north end of the camp had been wadded up in a ball and cast aside like aluminum foil. The area inside the fence was either charred or still on fire. I could make out where One-eyed Jack's squat should have been. The fence there was also destroyed, and so was a stretch of freeway on the other side.

A steady stream of ambulances was pulling away, and more were sitting in a line for their turn just outside the area.

"Father is waiting for us," Dierdre said. "He's located the summoning ritual site."

She drove on north a little way until we came to the railroad tracks. Pulling off onto the dirt, she stopped, and we got out.

"Up here. The sacrifice is different than before. The first one we found was a woman the city police identified as a prostitute. The next three were adult men."

I followed her, my stomach starting to do flip-flops. Off to the side of the tracks, we found Master Greenwood standing beside a double circle of black lines. In the middle was a body, spread-eagled and bloody.

It was Simone. I turned away and threw up. I hadn't cried in almost two years, but I felt tears running down my face. Dierdre hugged me, and pulled my hair back. Even after my stomach emptied, I continued to heave until it hurt.

"Here, drink this," Dierdre ordered. I took a couple of swallows from a water bottle she held out, and then threw it up. "Again." I followed her orders, and managed to keep it down that time.

"Did you know her?" she asked, her voice gentle.

"Yeah. Her name's Simone Dial. She's fifteen, a runaway from somewhere near Castle Rock. Her friends told me she disappeared two days ago." I shrugged away and sat down in the dirt. I stared at the horror in the circle for a couple of minutes. "A man picked her up and offered her a hundred dollars to go with him." I looked up at Dierdre. "A hooker the first time, you said? And now a street kid. I think they were probably easier than overpowering a full-grown man. But I'll bet the men were homeless as well."

"Was she a friend of yours?"

"Not really, but she was sweet, and kind. And if I ever find out who did this, the bastard will pay."

CHAPTER 23

The Greenwoods gave me a little time, then the Master asked, "Are you up to trying to track the summoner?"

I looked up from where I sat. "Don't you think it's a little suspicious that your asshole summoner decided to firebomb a homeless camp where a couple of your security personnel were beaten up last night?"

Dierdre cocked her head at me in that way she had, but her father just nodded. "It hadn't escaped my attention."

I got up and walked around the circle, searching for strange magic. I found it, along with Simone's residual life essence. Pivoting away, I followed the trail. As I expected, it soon ended at the street.

"This is where the car was parked," I said.

"So, that's it?" Dierdre asked.

"No, but we'll need to get a car to follow it."

The trail wasn't hard for me to follow, and we never got on a freeway. We were driving down a street with townhouses on either side when suddenly the trail was behind us.

"Woah! Pull over."

I got out and walked back until I found the car the summoner had used parked on the street. I followed his trail from there to a bus stop at the corner on the other side of the street.

"End of the line," I said.

"Where does this bus line go?" the Master asked.

"Downtown, Larimer Square, but if you transfer at the stadiums, you can get a bus to Carlisle Square."

"And we're back to the idea that the bastard is Guild," Dierdre said.

"That's my guess," I said.

"Or someone wants us to think he's a member of the Guild," the Master said.

We drove back to the Guild Hall and parked in the basement.

"The security people who were hurt at the homeless camp last night," I said. And when they turned to me, I continued, "Would it be possible to get pictures of them?"

"Yes," the Master answered. "Why?"

"Because I'd like to show them to Simone's friends. See if any of them were the man who took her."

He nodded. "I'll see you get them before you go."

I followed them onto the elevator, which took us to the third floor. We ended up in what I guessed was Master Greenwood's office. There was a desk next to a window with a view of Carlisle Square and the mountains in the distance. Books lined every wall, with a few paintings, and thick rugs covered the floor. A sitting area with heavy, cushioned chairs surrounded a low table.

The Master punched a button on the side of the table and said, "A cheeseboard for three, a bottle of Burgundy, and a pot of tea." Then he dropped into one of the chairs.

"A hell of a night," he said. "I hope I never see anything like that again."

Dierdre sat, so I did, also. They both looked tired and had an empty look in their eyes. I felt the same way.

"We didn't really stay at the camp very long," I said. "How bad was it?"

"More than a hundred people taken to hospital," Dierdre said. "No telling how many dead. I heard the cops say that normally there are between two hundred and three hundred people who camp there."

That tallied with my estimate. The shelters that the city and the churches provided were always full to capacity in the colder months. They didn't allow drugs and alcohol, so the camps such as that one attracted a lot of people.

"Did you ever stay there?" Dierdre asked.

I shook my head. "Not safe. A young girl would be asking for it. I don't drink much, and I never got into the drugs. The kids have their own camps. Ones that are easy to defend."

Her eyes widened slightly. "How so?"

"The camp I know the best is on the rooftop of an old warehouse. There's another one in a warehouse that's slated to be torn down, but the city and the owner have been arguing about who's going to pay for it. I've had an apartment since last fall. It's not much, but it's dry, warm, and safe. No one knows where I live."

There was a knock on the door, and a man brought in a large platter covered with various cheeses and toasted bread. There was also a bottle of wine with three glasses, and a tea service with three cups.

"I think it's remarkable that you've survived," Dierdre said after the man left.

I shrugged. "It's a jungle. Some people survive, others don't. Luck, as much as anything. And I've got my magic. Most don't."

"And that spelled *katana*," the Master said. "You took out Madeleine du Mont when she killed two master mages. You're young, but a half-grown lioness can be formidable."

He poured the wine, and I helped myself to the cheese board. I had never tasted some of the cheeses, and the marmalade beat the hell out of what they served in those little packets in diners. I wasn't much of a connoisseur of wines, either, but it was the best I'd ever tried.

We batted around ideas as to how to find the summoner—as well as the mages causing the other destruction—but after a while it felt like we were chasing our tails.

"If you can get me those pictures, I should go and see if anyone can identify them," I said.

Dierdre moved to the computer on the desk, and my phone pinged. I checked, and there were pictures of three men, all of whom looked to be in their thirties. One was the guy who followed me.

"Be careful," she said as I made ready to leave. "There's a big storm forecasted for tonight and tomorrow."

I had seen the warning on my phone. Spring in Colorado was usually an adventure. On my way out, I stopped by my room and grabbed my new ski parka. The forecast said four to fourteen inches of snow in town. I believed weathermen as much as I believed lawyers.

The street kids had also heard the weather warning. The rooftop camp was deserted. I hiked the extra six blocks to the old warehouse. There was a new chain-link fence surrounding the property, with 'No Trespassing' signs about every six feet.

It was a long slog around the fence to find where the kids had created an entrance. They hadn't cut the fence, but some debris had been piled up against it in one out-of-the-way corner. Some of the little ones might have had a problem with it on their own, but they were also the ones who could scamper up the chain link like climbing a ladder.

I first encountered a couple of older guys—seventeen or eighteen—and a girl about my age. One was armed with a club, and I saw the glint of light off the blade of a knife the girl held. All three had sharpened wooden stakes.

"It's Katy Brown," I called out. "No vampires."

The girl grinned. "Can't be too careful, ya know."

"I know it. Looking for a couple of young girls, Lisa and Caro. Last I saw them, they were crashing on the rooftop over on Crawford Street."

"Yeah, they're here."

The wind was picking up, blowing cold and promising worse. I made my way further into the warehouse, and up a set of stairs to the second floor. There were old offices there that were easier to heat, whether with a fire or just body heat. The first floor was too open to the wind.

They were sharing a room with three other girls older than they were. An old packing blanket covered the doorway, and it was relatively warm. It proved to be a fruitless trip.

"Naw, none of them," Lisa said. "He was tall, with long brown hair and a bushy beard. You didn't find her?"

I took a deep breath. "Yeah, I found her, but I was too late."

"She's dead?" Caro's voice shook.

"Yeah. You kids take care. Hear me? Take care of each other. Don't trust men, not even cops."

"We heard there was a big fire tonight at the camp near the mousetrap," Lisa said.

"Yes. Wiped it out. There will be more adults looking for a place after tonight. Be careful."

I wasn't near any bus routes that would take me home, so it was a long, cold hike. The temperature in my room wasn't much higher than outside, but at least it was out of the wind. I decided I had enough money to pay the heat bill, so I lit the little furnace and set it to low, then crawled into the blankets, and let the roaring wind lull me to sleep.

CHAPTER 24

It was quiet when I awoke. The wind had died down. I pulled back the blanket covering the dormer window and saw that the world was white and it was still snowing. Checking the weather on my phone, I found that snowfall totals in the metropolitan area varied from eight to twelve inches most places, with two feet in the foothills. Of course, when I had walked home the previous night, it was snowing sideways, so not much was sticking to the ground.

Such spring blizzards weren't common in Colorado, but they happened often enough that no one was surprised. The skiers would be happy, assuming their four-wheel drive vehicles could get through the drifts into the mountains. It was still below freezing, and I knew that when the clouds lifted, the temperature would plummet.

I didn't get in a hurry, turning up the heat, making tea, and taking a shower. There wasn't anything to eat. I hadn't been staying there often enough to stock the larder. The free food at the Guild Hall was all too alluring, and the cooks there were far better than I was.

After dressing in some of my new clothes—thermal underwear, two layers of socks, new hiking boots, and the ski parka—I ventured out. There was a snow shovel on the landing next to the back door, and when I opened the door, I was confronted with a three-foot drift. It took me about forty minutes to shovel off the stairs and reach the ground. After restoring the shovel to its normal place inside the locked door—ensuring that it was still available the next time I needed it—I set off into a world of white and quiet.

The snowplows had been working all night, but only the most major streets were cleared. Chances that the buses would be running were pretty slim, so I walked to a little Mexican diner about half a mile away. The food wasn't great, but it catered to cowboys and construction workers and had a parking lot. Sure enough, there were lots of four-by-four pickups parked around it, and the place was crowded.

I waited until someone finished eating at the counter, and took his place. The coffee was strong and black, and the *huevos rancheros* with beans and rice filled me up. I sat there with my second cup of coffee, trying to figure out what to do with my day.

The burned-out camp under the interchange would be buried in snow, and the authorities probably weren't in a major hurry to sort it out. Likewise the summoning place. I assumed Simone's body had been taken to the Hall. There wasn't any point in trying to check on Lisa and Caro. I knew no one at that old warehouse had gone out into the storm the night before, and they weren't likely to that morning.

I was curious about Loretta Lighthorse. Maybe teaming up with another tracker *was* a good idea. She had said she was a friend of Morgan's, and I knew where he lived.

"Do you think it's okay to ask if anyone is going out to Glendale?" I asked the waitress. "My car isn't going to get me to work in this mess, and the buses aren't running."

She shrugged. "Doesn't hurt to try." She stood on her tiptoes and yelled, "Anyone going to Glendale? This young lady needs a ride to work."

In short order, a cowboy-looking guy volunteered. His truck was a huge four-by-four and didn't look as though it was used for any kind of cowboy-type work. Colorado status symbol. He dropped me off on Colorado Boulevard in Glendale, and I walked through the snow to Morgan's apartment building. Some businesses had shoveled their walks, but few people in the residential areas had.

I always thought that, for a country boy, Morgan's choice of home was rather odd. He rented a two-bedroom apartment on the fifth floor of a high-rise apartment building in Glendale, a tiny city of its own in the middle of Queen City. It was mostly apartment and office buildings, and attracted a yuppie population. Of course, the single women lounging by the swimming pool in summer probably hooked him.

I got off the elevator, walked down the hallway, and pressed his buzzer. Then I waited. I knew he was there because his silver pickup—half buried in snow—was in the parking lot.

He opened the door after the third time I pressed the call button. He was wearing a bathrobe, and toweling his wet hair.

"Yeah? Oh, hi, Katy. Come in."

He poured me a cup of coffee, and I watched the snow out the window, trying to make it plain that I wasn't interested in playing any naked games. He got the hint and went into the bedroom to dress.

"So, what brings you out on this beautiful spring morning?"

"Research. I had someone offer to team up with me, and she said she's a friend of yours."

"Oh? And who might that be?"

"Loretta Lighthorse."

"Ah. Yes, I guess you could call us friends. I've known her a long time. Went to school with her."

"She's Native American?"

"Yeah. Her mother was. Died in childbirth, so Loretta was raised by her grandparents. I think her father was a mage, but he didn't stick around."

"Could he have been a vampire?"

Morgan shot me a look, then said, "Vampires can't have kids."

I explained the circumstances that could lead to the birth of a dhampir. According to what I could find in the Guild archives, their mothers always died in childbirth.

"Well, I know that she has some magic, but not sure exactly what," he continued. "She's a good tracker, can handle herself in a fight. A little unconventional. She prefers to stake a vampire with a bow. Makes her own wooden arrows."

That would be handy. Without my shield, I wouldn't want to get within arm's reach of a vampire.

"Is she honest? Trustworthy?" I asked.

He gave a slight shrug, then looked me straight in the eye. "As much as any of us are. She won't try to cheat you out of a bounty, and she'll split one if that's the deal. I don't think she'd run out on you in a fight, or use you for bait without telling you. Is that what you want to know?"

"Did you ever sleep with her?" I asked.

"Once. A long time ago. We aren't a good match."

"She didn't try to drink your blood?"

Morgan chuckled and shook his head. "I think she's into some kinky shit, but I didn't stick around long enough to explore all her kinks. She may be into that."

Morgan was a romantic, drawn to Audrey Hepburn movies and taking care of someone. I doubted Loretta thought she needed a protector, or would be happy keeping house.

"One warning," Morgan said. "She's into women as well as men, and ex-lovers can be tricky. Katy, if you're going to partner with someone, with another tracker, get a contract. Talk to Don Treadle, the bartender at the Tracker's Lounge. He can recommend a lawyer to draw one up."

CHAPTER 25

The contract sounded like a good idea, but the idea of legal ties led me to think about what kind of legal obligations I might have to the Guild. They were feeding and housing me, and I now had an account in their own bank, where they were depositing 500 dollars a week.

So, that gave me three people to talk to, and I wasn't sure if there was a particular order in which I should do that. I assumed Dierdre stayed at the Hall the previous night. The Tracker's Lounge might or might not be even open with all the snow, and Don Treadle might or might not have made it into work. Morgan didn't know where Loretta lived, and didn't have her phone number. They might have been friends, but obviously not close friends.

The snow had let up by the time I left Morgan's, and I talked him into giving me a ride to Carlisle Square. Unfortunately, I didn't think that one through, and had to help him dig out his pickup.

On our way downtown, I asked him, "What do you make of all these weird events? You know, tornadoes, earthquakes, demons."

"Mages playing games. People are saying the Guild's lost control. Maybe time for a change in leadership, or maybe reorganize and rethink the entire thing. I mean, the Guild is supposed to keep that kind of crap from happening, right?"

"That's what everyone has always told me."

He shook his head. "I'm not going to stick around to find out. End of the month, I'm pulling out and heading to Dallas. The problems they're having down there with the vamps and weres going after each other is generating a demand for trackers, and they're paying large bounties. You're welcome to come with me, if you want to."

As if jumping in the middle of a supernatural war was better than what was going on in Queen City. If he'd suggested Hawaii, or a fishing cabin thirty miles from the nearest town—one with two bedrooms with locking doors—I might have considered it.

"Thanks, but I think I'll ride it out here a little longer. I don't think this problem is going to continue."

"Suit yourself. I'll send you my address once I get settled."

He dropped me off, and I walked across Carlisle Square, which was completely clear of snow. There wasn't even any snow piled up around the edges, unlike other places. The steps of the Guild Hall were clear and dry. One might think they used magic. I doubted there was a snow shovel in the entire building. That was some magic I wanted to learn.

Dierdre was in her office.

"I take it you stayed here last night," I said.

"Yes, and I don't know why you didn't. It must have been a cold walk home."

"I had to let Simone's friends know about her."

I saw Dierdre's face soften, and her eyes got a little misty. She nodded.

"I have an idea for a lesson today," I said.

"Oh?"

"I want to know how you cleared all that snow."

She threw back her head and laughed.

"You may think it's funny, but it took me forty minutes to clear the snow off the stairs at my place," I said.

"Well, I can show you how to do it using rune magic. But you'll probably figure out a better way using your threads."

We took the elevator down to the basement and transported out to the Farm. It didn't have as much snow as the city, which was closer to the mountains. It was my first lesson in linking runes. Dierdre showed me one rune to melt the snow, and another one to evaporate the resulting water. Then she linked them together and triggered them.

"By linking the runes in this particular sequence, you provide one magical input to execute the desired event," she said.

It took me a couple of times to get it right, and I still wasn't as smooth as she was, but it worked. I was smiling so hard my face almost hurt.

When we got back to her office, I broached the idea of me teaming up with Loretta Lighthorse.

"I had another tracker approach me about teaming up to find the summoner. She's magical in some way, but I'm not sure how, and she's registered with the Guild, I assume, since she's collected bounties."

Dierdre lifted one eyebrow. "Name?'

I told her, and she swiveled to her computer and typed. After reading whatever came up on the screen, she typed some more.

"Interesting," was her comment.

"Another tracker, someone who mentored me a bit, said I should do a contract. Make sure what we were doing—and not doing—was clear for all parties. But I didn't want to do anything that violated my obligations to the Guild."

"I don't think there would be any, but I'd like Dad to review the contract before you sign it. He's a lot more familiar with our association with the trackers."

"Sure, I can do that."

As I was getting off the elevator prior to leaving the building, I ran into one of my least favorite people—Master Rathske, the person in charge of the Guild's bounty operation. The first time I met him, he suggested that I could become his apprentice.

He often told me how much I resembled my mother. While that was true, the way he said it made me wonder if he'd had the hots for her. The leer and the way he scoped out my body gave me a pretty good idea of what he expected from an apprentice, and I declined. I was fourteen the first time he made his offer, and I had no clue how old he was. He could have been Master Greenwood's brother. Both were tall, with shoulder-length brown hair, and beards that reached their chests. Rathske was younger and slimmer. He wasn't bad to look at—rather handsome, actually—but he gave me the creeps.

"Kaitlyn." He seemed surprised to see me. "What are you doing here?"

"Uh, I work here. I'm apprenticed to Dierdre Greenwood."

The expression on his face changed to disappointed, almost angry.

"And what brought this about? I've offered you such an opportunity more than once. I think I'm more qualified to mentor a tracker than she is."

"Master Greenwood set it up."

The storm on his face moved from slightly overcast to full-blown natural disaster. His jaw muscles worked, and it seemed like he wanted to say something, or bite something, but couldn't decide which. His face seemed to swell as it turned red. I decided it was time to go.

"Well, it's nice running into you again," I said. "Got to go."

I turned and headed across the wide lobby toward the doors. The strides I took were such that he would have had to run to catch up with me, and I figured he wouldn't abandon his dignity. Pushing through the main doors, out into brilliant sunlight and fresh air, I heaved a sigh of relief.

Although the snow had been cleared from Carlisle Square, it hadn't been in most other places, and the day was brighter than summer. The major streets were clear, and the buses were running on those routes. I grabbed one that dropped me off near the Tracker's Lounge.

The path to the front door had been shoveled, a distinct improvement on many of the surrounding sidewalks. I had to chuckle that a bar was open while the grocery store down the street was still dark.

Sometimes the world is entirely inscrutable, and sometimes it seems filled with wondrous magic. The only two people in the bar were Loretta Lighthorse and Don Treadle.

I sat down at the bar next to Loretta, and Don poured me an ale without me ordering. I reflected that maybe I was a little young to be a regular in a bar. I pushed a five across the bar, and he made it disappear.

Turning to her, I said, "I've been thinking about your offer. There were friends of mine in that homeless camp, and no one seems to be any closer to finding the summoner."

She nodded. "What kind of bounty do you think the Guild will pay?"

"No idea."

"You could probably name your price," Don said. "I would think six figures wouldn't be out of the question."

"Morgan said we should sign a contract."

Before Loretta could say anything, Don said, "Good idea. I can recommend a lawyer."

He made a phone call and came back, handing each of us a business card.

"He said to come around Thursday afternoon, at about four."

CHAPTER 26

Loretta and I sat at a corner table, and I told her everything I knew about the demon manifestations. The places and rituals used to summon it, and my connection to the homeless camp it had ravaged. I also told her about the speculations of the Greenwoods.

In turn, she told me of the rumors and speculations she was aware of.

"So," she said, "do you have any plan for finding this summoner? Any ideas for a trap we could lay for him or her?"

I shook my head. "No. What I do know is that he's getting his victims off the street—homeless people and hookers. The events are random, and I can't shake the feeling that the other destructive events—the tornado, the super Chinook, the earthquake—are tied to it."

"The snowstorm?"

Again, I shook my head. "This happens often enough that no one thinks it's anything but natural. And it's not localized. They got twice this much snow in the mountains. Besides, from what I know, weather manipulation on that scale is an extremely rare talent."

She nodded. "Okay. You say Master Greenwood thinks this is an assault on the credibility of the Guild. You also mentioned that it felt like teenage vandalism. I think that's closer, although it's going to have an effect on the Guild and its relationship with the wider community. I think what we have is a chaos mage. Someone doing these things not just for the sheer hell of it, but with the aim of tearing apart the system."

"What's that?" I asked. "A chaos mage?"

She didn't answer immediately. Then, with a deep sigh—something I was used to when an adult figured out how ignorant I was—she said, "The world, people, magic exist on a continuum between order and chaos. The Guild's stated mission is to maintain balance. Perfect order isn't attainable, and no one would want that anyway. But chaos is something most people don't want, either. Imagine if you couldn't depend on anything. Nothing occurred on an expected schedule. Clocks showed random times—none of them the same. People just acted on impulse, and society— Well, there wouldn't be any society. No cops. No Guild. If you could protect yourself, you'd have a chance, but otherwise, there would be nothing to stop someone from beating you, raping you, killing you."

That sounded awfully familiar. The life of a street kid.

"But why would a mage want that?" I asked.

"Power. Sheer sadism. Mental instability. Hell, I don't know, but there are a lot of strange people out there. Why can't vamps and weres abide by the rules? But there are mages like that, and they are the enemies of the Guild."

"So, you're saying that such a person isn't just trying to take over the Guild, they're trying to take it down."

She nodded. "Exactly. But I would think the Guild would be aware of such a possibility and have anyone with that inclination under observation. Maybe it's someone who has recently come to Queen City."

"Someone who isn't a member of the Guild—someone they

don't know about." I thought about it for a moment, then said, "To be aware of something, you have to acknowledge its probability, its existence," I said. "The mundanes ignore magic most of the time because it's uncomfortable. The Guild might be that way toward a chaos mage. They might even have suspicions, but they brush them away because they don't want to think about it."

"That's true. But how could you and I access their records? The clues might be there in someone's personnel file, but we'll never see it. And unless they decide to look, it's just speculation by a couple of outsiders." She gave me a quirky little grin. "Unless one of your Guild friends helps us."

I shrugged. "Doesn't hurt to ask."

I took myself back to the Guild Hall and went looking for Dierdre. She wasn't in her office, but I did find Marlene.

"Hey," I said, dropping into the chair in front of her desk. "How much do you know about this demon problem?"

She shook her head. "Not a whole lot. The Master and Dierdre have been working with you on that."

The tone in her voice and her stiff posture made me think she felt excluded.

"I don't think that they're intentionally excluding you," I said. "I was going to talk with Dierdre, but she's not available. Perhaps you can help me out. Someone made the suggestion that a chaos mage was to blame for the demon and the other problems. You know, the earthquake and that stuff."

She leaned back in her chair and looked thoughtful. I waited a moment, then said, "I'm not real clear on the whole order versus chaos thing. I guess it's like two sides of the same coin?"

"Oh, no. It isn't either or, it's a continuum. Total order for a human society would look like an anthill, or a beehive. Everyone has their place, their role, they carry it out, and the whole thing is clockwork. But humans aren't like that, are they? They get creative, they screw up, they rebel. Imagine if every day had the same weather, the same temperature, it rained only between 3:15 and 4:15, and it was the same in January as in June. But the world doesn't work that way, does it? It's infinitely variable."

She took a sip from the mug on her desk. "On the other hand, total chaos would mean you wouldn't be able to count on anything. Not only wouldn't the buses run on time, it would be anyone's guess if they ran at all—and for how long. You couldn't count on any kind of norms. You couldn't count on anything working the way it was supposed to. Will there be food today? Will water appear when you turn on the tap? Maybe, maybe not. With total anarchy, the strongest, most violent would rule, and with total capriciousness. Do you see what I mean?"

"Sounds like my life before I came here."

The intensity melted from her face, and her eyes kind of filmed over. "Dierdre said you were living on the streets."

"Not anymore, but I did for a while. Working as a tracker gave me enough money to rent a room. Rogue vamps, kidnapped kids, lost dogs—I can find them. But there are a lot of people who don't have magic, don't have any skills, and have nowhere to go. They're prey, and there are plenty of predators."

"And it would be worse without the Guild," she said. "We try to control the chaos, try find balance."

She pursed her lips and rolled her eyes up to the ceiling, then said, "Yeah, a chaos mage would explain a lot."

A while later, Marlene was drilling me on linking runes when Dierdre dropped by. We told her about Loretta's theory.

"That does make some sense," she said. "I'll mention it to Dad."

CHAPTER 27

As the skies cleared, the temperature plummeted into the single digits. After dinner that evening, I stuck my nose outside and immediately turned around. I spent the night in my cozy room at the Guild Hall.

When I went downstairs to have breakfast, the TV in the café was broadcasting the news about the events from the previous evening. There had been another demon manifestation, and it had destroyed the Governor's Mansion before going on to wreak havoc on the surrounding blocks. Luckily, the governor and his family weren't home, but five people there lost their lives. The remarkable thing was that a television station had caught the demon on camera. It looked exactly like the one from previous incidents.

A guy in a suit—evidently a state legislator from the opposition party—was ranting about magic users and saying it was time to round them all up and stick them on reservations where they could hurt only each other.

"The Lord has told us to suffer not a witch to live!" he practically shouted before the show moved on to something else. I had read about the Witch Wars in history books. I couldn't imagine that someone would want to start that all over again, but demons weren't a trivial matter.

I accompanied Dierdre and Master Greenwood to the Governor's Mansion. For the first time, Marlene went with us. The State Police had already identified the summoning site, which was in the park or garden directly behind the mansion. They had also identified the sacrifice victim, who had a history of arrests for prostitution.

She had been mutilated like the other victims. Pretty—except for the way terror and pain had twisted her features—and she couldn't have been older than twenty-one. I took one glance and didn't look at her again. Marlene threw up.

The demon's trail led directly from the circle to the mansion. It was obvious that the building was the summoner's target. The devastation continued on the north side toward the Capitol, but after wiping out most of four blocks, and killing another twenty people, the demon had disappeared.

The summoner had exited the park and departed from the scene in some sort of vehicle. That was the first break we'd had, and I spent the day tracking it. Dierdre drove me, stopping when I asked her to so that I could sniff around.

"Is that much mutilation necessary for a summoning?" I asked as we drove.

"I don't think so," Dierdre said. "The heart torn from the chest is kind of classic. A reward for the demon. But disemboweling the victim while she's still awake? I think that's pure sadism. We have established that the sacrifices were drugged, but probably not enough to knock them out."

It was mid-afternoon when we found the car. The license plate was missing, as were the manufacturer's vehicle identification numbers. The police later told us the car had been reported stolen that morning.

The vehicle's occupant had walked across a school ground and caught a bus on the other side. Dead end again.

"He's playing with us," I said. "Laughing his ass off. We just chased all over town only to end up at another bus stop."

"Is there any pattern you can see with the buses he's taking?" she asked.

I shook my head. "It really doesn't matter. Once you're on a bus, you can transfer and transfer until you get to where you want to go. There's another bus stop two blocks over, going the opposite direction." I tried to think. "Maybe if I brought in a friend of mine. Jodi's like a math prodigy, you know? She knows more about the bus routes and schedules than the city's computers do."

"Might be worth bringing her in. We'll pay her for her time."

That would guarantee Jodi's help. I asked Dierdre to drop me off at the lawyer's office so I could meet with him and Loretta.

"Do you want me to wait for you?"

"No. I'll try and find Jodi afterward. I'll see you tomorrow."

The lawyer had a draft contract that he gave each of us.

"Read them over, fill in the blanks where you can, and decide if there is anything additional that I need to add or anything you want changed," he said. "Bring them back on Tuesday, and we'll make the changes, sign it, and I'll file it for you."

He said the total cost was one hundred fifty bucks. I looked at Loretta, and she shrugged.

We left his office, and I hitched a ride with her to the knitting shop on Lipan. I walked up to the shop in a residential neighborhood. The sign over the door in about six different colored letters read, 'DYI Dry Goods' and underneath in smaller letters, 'Knitting and Quilting Supplies.'

The house was similar to the rest of those on the street—small clapboard two-story painted white. I pushed the door open and a bell jangled. A rather large woman—tall and solid, but not fat—with very short hair and a bright smile, stood behind the counter. Jodi was closer to me, unloading a box full of skeins of wool and putting them on a shelf. The store itself was a riot of color, with wool stacked on shelves around the room. A low doorway led to another room with quilts hanging from the ceiling.

It was the first time I'd seen Jodi since I learned to see auras. Hers was a bonfire. I'd never seen an aura so hot, not even at the Guild Hall. I stared with my mouth gaping open.

Jodi's eyes grew large when she saw me, and I saw her furtive glance toward the woman behind the counter.

"May I help you?" the woman behind the counter asked.

"Wow!" I said. "This place is impressive!"

The woman's smile widened. "What can I help you with?"

"I actually came to see Jodi," I answered. "My boss has some short-term work that needs a lot of number crunching. I said I might know someone who can do it."

The woman raised an eyebrow, then looked toward Jodi. "She's certainly good with numbers. Who's your friend, Jodi?"

"I'm Katy Brown," I said. "Jodi and I used to look after each other." I figured the woman knew at least some of Jodi's story.

"And this is Delia Gosling," Jodi said. "She's my foster mom."

I knew they had to have some sort of story they told people, and 'this is the pedophile who keeps me off the streets' wasn't something you told customers.

I smiled at Delia. "I'm glad Jodi found a good place." I looked around. "Feels very comfy."

"How much work are you talking about?" Delia asked. "And how much does it pay?"

"Probably two or three hours a day for the next couple of weeks. It pays twenty dollars an hour." That part was a lie. Dierdre had said she would pay thirty-five, but I wanted to make sure Jodi came away with some cash even if her 'foster mom' wanted a cut.

"Well, I have no objection. Give you a little pocket money?" She looked at Jodi.

"Sure, that will work. I already finished the taxes and stuff, and I'm all caught up on the daily books."

Delia Gosling was no fool. Stocking shelves was one thing, but having Jodi do her books showed an awareness of the girl's true value.

"I can come by and get you tomorrow," I said. "About nine o'clock?"

"Yeah, sure. That'll be fine," Jodi said.

CHAPTER 28

On our way to the Guild Hall the following morning, I filled Jodi in on our problem. When I mentioned that our suspected summoner was using the bus system to confound trackers, she perked up.

"You want to know where he's going, right? Yeah, I can compute some probabilities. Those are fun!"

I knew Dierdre would love her.

When we arrived at the Hall, I found that I didn't have the authority to sign her into the building. Dierdre came down to do that, and I saw from the glances she gave Jodi that she had some reservations about relying on someone so young.

In a conference room next to her office, she had a large map of the city spread out on a big table. All the bus routes and stops were indicated, and the locations of the summoning rituals were marked, along with the bus stops I had identified as getaway spots.

Jodi studied the map, walking around the table to look at it from different angles.

"Can I get you something to drink?" Marlene asked.

"Oh, sure. Do you have a Coke?"

Pretty soon, Jodi asked for paper and a pencil. Marlene brought them, and Dierdre said, "We can provide a computer or anything else you need. I have this same map on the computer."

"Oh, maybe I can use that," Jodi said, "but it's a lot slower than doing the calculations on paper. I don't type very well."

From that point on, we all shut up and just watched. Dierdre drew me off to the side.

"Have you looked at her aura?" she asked.

"Yeah, pretty spectacular, huh?"

Dierdre shook her head. "I'm surprised she doesn't combust."

"Oh, I've seen that. A guy tried to get too familiar. But she tries to avoid that because it burns off all her clothes."

My boss stared at me with her mouth open. "Has she had any training?"

"Nope."

"We can't just let her run around like that. Teenage hormones and emotions—hell, she could set the whole city on fire."

"Uh, well, she's a bit skittish as far as the Guild is concerned. And I'm sure her foster mom would throw a fit."

Jodi pored over the map and scribbled on the paper we gave her for about three hours. Then we took her down to the cafeteria and fed her a hamburger.

"What next?" Dierdre asked. "Are you making any progress?"

"I think so. I need to stop by the library and get a book."

"A book on what?"

"Chaos theory. I've never really studied it, but I wonder if it might be helpful."

I set down my iced tea. "What is chaos theory?"

I knew immediately that I shouldn't have asked. Jodi got very animated.

"It's a method of analysis into the behavior of dynamic systems that can't be explained or predicted by single data relationships. It requires whole, continuous data relationships, and focuses on underlying patterns and deterministic laws of dynamical systems that are highly sensitive to initial conditions."

My face must have mirrored my blank mind.

"It's a branch of mathematics," she said.

"Whatever helps," Dierdre said, and I could tell she was as lost as I was. She paid Jodi for the day, and Marlene gave her a ride to the main library and dropped her off.

⁂

When I swung by the knitting shop to get her the following morning, she had a large book more than two inches thick.

"Chaos theory?" I asked.

"Yup."

"We were hoping you could help us a little quicker than that."

She gave me a smug smile and a wink. "Read half of it last night. Just getting into the fun part—the mathematics. That might take me another evening or two. But the author has a website, and we can download templates for his mathematical models. All we have to do is load our data and then start playing what-if games. Do they have internet at the Guild Hall?"

I wasn't as blown away as Dierdre was. I'd known for a long time that Jodi was special.

Marlene downloaded the templates Jodi wanted, ran the Guild's standard scans on them to make sure they were safe, then loaded them into a section of the main computer Dierdre had requisitioned for the project.

"Is that like a super computer or something?" I asked.

"Or something," Marlene replied. "It's an array of extremely powerful servers the Guild chapters fund at a center near Washington D.C. I have some alerts set up, and if another set of disasters similar to ours happens anywhere, we'll be notified."

"Just because we believe in magic doesn't mean we don't use technology when it's needed," Dierdre said with a grin.

Jodi spent most of the day working with the models, projecting their outputs onto the map Dierdre had on the computer. Then she would clear out the whole thing and do it again a bit differently. My understanding of computers basically started and ended with searching the internet at the library and reading what I found, so I was no help at all. And bored, to tell the truth.

***

The following morning, Jodi and I were on the bus when the earthquake hit. She rode it out hanging onto the seat in front of her. I landed on my ass in the aisle. The driver did fairly well, but he sideswiped a couple of cars before he could wrestle the bus to a stop.

When the world stopped moving, we hiked the rest of the way to the Guild Hall. To my surprise, there didn't seem to be much damage at Carlisle Square. One building that had been damaged by the first quake had collapsed, and maybe there were a few more cracks in other buildings, but the large cracks in the square that had come with the first quake were absent.

"Maybe it wasn't as bad as the first one?" Jodi suggested.

"I don't know. It lasted longer. I think it was farther away, maybe?"

A TV in the cafeteria usually was tuned to the news, but it showed only static when we popped in so I could grab some breakfast.

Dierdre seemed always to be in her office, and that's where we found her.

"Do you even feel the earthquakes in here?" I asked.

She shrugged. "Not the shaking, but we do get a little of the rockin' and rollin'. I'm sure there will be more strengthening of the wards. Some of the people here would rather bury their heads in the sand and strengthen our defenses rather than put any effort into catching the bastard who's doing this."

I shook my head. "Do you really still think only one person is involved? I mean, how many mages have the strength to cause an earthquake that large?"

"Not too many," Master Greenwood's voice came from behind me. "It would be an impressive feat even for a circle of three. If anyone has any business on the west side of the city, I suggest you plan your route carefully. The freeway collapsed just past Sheridan Boulevard, as did one of the on-ramps at Federal."

"So, we're looking for a gang," I said.

He nodded. "Unfortunately, I think so. The demon summoner may be involved with the other disasters, but I find it difficult to believe that a geomancer also has the power to cause tornados. And as far as this earthquake is concerned, there aren't many mages in the world who have that much power."

"Are any of them here in Queen City?" I asked, and he shrugged, which scared the hell out of me. "As I said, a geomancer as the focus of a circle could pull it off."

He fixed his gaze on Jodi. "Come here, child."

She shuffled toward him, obviously reluctant, and he knelt down in front of her. "I'm Elias Greenwood. Would you like to learn about your abilities?"

Jodi stared at him, her eyes wide, and then slowly nodded her head.

"We can test you and find out exactly what your talents are," he said. "You can ask Kaitlyn, it doesn't hurt at all, and it doesn't obligate you to anything." He smiled. "Contrary to what some people say, the Guild doesn't force mages to join. But I think that you have power that scares you sometimes, don't you?"

She reluctantly nodded again.

"We can teach you how to control it."

"I—I would like that."

"When we sort out our current problems, tell Kaitlyn when you're ready, and we'll set up for the testing, okay?"

Jodi returned to her computer monitor, and I looked up at Master Greenwood.

"You aren't scary at all, sometimes," I blurted out.

He smiled, chuckled, and looked toward Dierdre. "I have some experience with little girls."

CHAPTER 29

I was in the mood for fish and chips, and getting away from the Guild Hall for a while, so I told Jodi I'd buy her dinner at Two Fools.

We were halfway across the expanse of the lobby, heading for the outside doors, when Master Rathske intercepted us.

"Hello, Kaitlyn! How are you doing? I notice that you haven't been collecting any bounties lately. Is that because Master Greenwood has you too busy with your studies, or perhaps he's using your talents in other ways. Tracking down demon summoners, perhaps?"

"Oh, well, yes. My studies for sure. I have a lot of catching up to do."

"And who is your friend?"

Although Rathske was talking to me, he never really looked at me. He was staring at Jodi the way a starving man looked at food.

"Oh, this is Jodi," I said. "She's an old friend of mine."

"Hello, Jodi. I don't believe I've seen you here before. Are you a new student?"

When Rathske first stopped us, Jodi took a step back, and

was standing sort of behind me. I could feel the tension radiating from her.

"She's not a student," I said. "She's just setting up some testing to determine her talents."

"Well, Jodi, young mages can benefit from having a personal mentor. I happen to have the time to provide tutoring for a young mage with promise. My name is Master Rathske. Any time you need anything, or have any questions, feel free to come and see me. My office is over there," he pointed in the direction of the bounty desk to the side of the lobby. The official name was Paranormal Incidents Department.

"Oh, well, that's very generous of you," I said. "We need to catch a bus. Her mom will be worried if we're late."

Spinning away from him, I grabbed Jodi's arm and pulled her along toward the doors. The poor kid was practically running to keep up with me. Once outside, I let go of her.

"If that son of a bitch ever touches me, I'll light him up like a Roman candle," Jodi said, her face twisted in an expression of disgust. "Mentor my ass."

"That's exactly what he wants to mentor. Yeah, not one of my favorite people. He likes young girls."

One thing I had done while talking with Rathske was touch the ley line and look at his aura. Dark brown, bordered with black, and very strong. He was a geomancer. I wondered if Master Greenwood had him on a suspect list.

We caught the bus, and with one transfer, landed at Two Fools. It wasn't too crowded, and as I looked around for a table, I saw someone waving at me—Loretta Lighthorse. I led Jodi over to the booth.

"Hey, come join me," Loretta said.

I let Jodi slide into the other side of the booth, then sat beside her.

"Loretta, this is my friend Jodi. Loretta is another tracker."

Jodi was a lot friendlier to Loretta than she had been to Rathske, but still reticent.

"Hi," she said, then pulled a menu in front of her face and studied it.

Loretta smiled slightly, then said, "What did you think of our latest earthquake?"

"A definite surprise," I said. "I've lived here my whole life, and never felt an earthquake until recently."

She nodded. "I talked to a friend who teaches at a university in California. He says these quakes aren't natural."

It was pretty obvious that she wanted me to respond to that, but the waitress showed up with water for Jodi and me. We ordered our dinners, and after the waitress walked away, I found that Loretta was still watching my face with that expectant air.

"The city administration seems to think they're magically caused," I said.

"And possibly tied to the demons and tornados and other mischief?"

I reluctantly nodded. "But even more difficult to track."

"Not necessarily. The spell caster has to be fairly close to the event. I mean, your friend might be able to set this block on fire, but I don't think she can start a fire in the mountains from here."

Jodi's head jerked up, and I realized that Loretta was able to read auras.

"But the problem we've had with the demon summonings is that by the time the manifestation occurs, the summoner has escaped. Why wouldn't it be the same for someone starting an earthquake?" I asked. "So far, no one has sent the Guild advanced notice of the events."

"And even if you got there ahead of time," Jodi piped up, "you don't know who you're looking for, so he could walk right by you."

"Master Greenwood thinks it's more than one person," I said. "He suggested the possibility of a circle."

Loretta looked thoughtful at that, and still hadn't responded by the time the waitress brought our dinners. Jodi dug into her bangers and mash, and I popped a still-too-hot fry in my mouth.

"I think the idea of a circle would eliminate the idea of a chaos mage," Loretta said. "So, what other motives would someone have to do all this crap?"

Jodi shook her head. "A chaos affiliation doesn't mean the mage's thought processes are unorganized. Look, what we're looking for is a sociopath. Whether his or her motive is chaos, revenge, or acquiring power is irrelevant. It's a powerful mage who doesn't give a damn about anyone but himself. He doesn't give a thought about killing people, wrecking their homes, ruining their lives. And sociopaths will use people, so I don't think we can discount the idea of a circle or a gang with different talents."

Loretta looked at her in surprise. I chuckled.

"She may be young, but she ain't dumb," I said.

Loretta snorted. "Neither are you. So, where does that leave us?"

"We need the Guild to tell us about their sociopaths, as well as any sociopaths they know of who aren't in the Guild," Jodi said, shoving a fork full of food into her mouth.

"Good luck with that," Loretta said. "The Guild is full of arrogant narcissists. There can be a fine line between that and a sociopath."

CHAPTER 30

It was late when Jodi and I left the pub, and I had an uneasy feeling—nothing I could put my finger on, but I was uncomfortable. There was a strong wind—although not of the super-Chinook mage-driven strength—so, instead of taking Jodi home, I took her back to the Guild Hall with me.

The reception desk at the Paranormal Incidents Department seemed busy. Since so much of what they did was involved with vampires and werewolves, the desk was staffed all night. The presence of Master Rathske, standing by the desk, wasn't usual, though. He was rarely there after dark, preferring his mansion in the foothills, which I assumed was more conducive to 'mentoring' the young girls who struck his fancy.

He watched us cross the lobby to the elevators, and when the doors closed, he was still watching us.

The intercom in my room woke me in the morning.

"Kaitlyn! Get up! The demon is loose again!" Dierdre's voice.

I roused Jodi.

"Hey, kid, up and at 'em. Let's go catch a demon summoner."

We dressed and hit the cafeteria for breakfast sandwiches on our way down to the parking level. Dierdre and her father were waiting for us.

As we climbed into the car, Dierdre turned to us in the back seat and said, "Jodi, do you need any of the maps or the calculations you've been doing?"

"Nah, I've got it all in my head."

Dierdre glanced at me and I nodded. "If she says she does, she does."

"Is there anything you can't do?" Dierdre said with a grin.

"Cook. For some reason, if you put me in a kitchen with a bunch of ingredients, I get confused. Show me a recipe, and I remember it, but there's always too much going on at once. I can cook eggs, and I can cook pancakes, but not at the same time. Delia gave up trying to teach me. The only thing I'm allowed to do in the kitchen now is make tea."

"Where are we going?" I asked as Dierdre accelerated up the ramp out of the parking garage.

"Downtown," her father said. "The demon was first reported near Lincoln Park, headed toward the Capitol."

"What time is it?" I asked.

"Nine-fifteen," Jodi answered. She wasn't wearing a watch, and didn't have a cell phone, but I took her word for it.

"It was first sighted about an hour ago," Master Greenwood said, "and it's been making its way northeast since then."

"Has it reached the river yet?"

"I don't know. It seems to be moving rather slowly and destroying everything in its path."

"That's near Delia's shop," Jodi said to me under her breath.

The demon was in the process of crossing the 13th Street bridge when we arrived at the river. Two police armored assault vehicles blocked its path on the east side. They opened fire at it with machine guns on the roofs of the vehicles. As far as I could see, the demon didn't even slow down.

Some sort of rocket was fired at it and scored a direct hit. The demon rocked back on its heels, but otherwise, didn't seem to be affected.

Dierdre pulled the car over to the curb, and she and the Master got out. I followed them, and Jodi followed me.

The demon reached the armored trucks and swatted one with its hand. The truck crashed over on its side on the concrete embankment, half hanging over the river. Then the demon kicked the other truck, and it did a one-and-a-half back-flip, landing on its top. The cops that were massed behind the trucks ran in every direction, but I didn't have a good feeling about the men inside.

Master Greenwood walked toward the bridge, raising his arms. The river seemed to rise, and rise, forming a wave in the air, and pouring down onto the bridge and the demon. It let out a deafening growl—almost a scream. A cloud of steam rose into the air and spread out, creating a fog that completely hid the bridge from view.

Dierdre grabbed my arm and pulled me toward her.

"Go! Track the damned thing. Find the summoner!" she yelled over the din. She let go of me and walked up behind her father, laying her hand on his shoulder. The river continued to pour over the bridge.

Easy for her to say. There was a pissed off demon standing in the middle of the track I was supposed to follow.

I grabbed Jodi. "Go back to the car and stay there. Either that or go to the knitting shop."

I let go of her and took off running. The nearest bridge was 14th Street, and I had to get across the river before I could pick up the demon's trail. There were cops everywhere, and they had closed off the area. Since I was running away from the action, no one tried to stop me.

The 14th Street bridge was also closed, so I didn't have any traffic to contend with. I leaped over the barricade and dashed onto the bridge. I heard shouts to stop, but I kept going. At the other end, a couple of cops tried to grab me, so I shielded and slipped by them.

When I reached 13th Street, I stopped to catch my breath. The east end of the bridge was shrouded in a steamy fog. I couldn't see the demon, but I could definitely tell he had passed that way. The stench was almost overwhelming.

The cops had the east end of the bridge blocked, but I wasn't going that direction. I turned and headed along the path of destruction. No one needed a tracker to figure out where the demon had come from. In addition to the stench—both magical and olfactory—the trail looked like pictures I'd seen of bombed cities. Damaged buildings and rubble everywhere.

There were bodies, not all of them dead, and I passed a few ambulances and paramedics trying to help the injured.

It wasn't easy going. I had to slow down due to the rubble. The demon had taken a straight path, directly through buildings, trees, cars, and anything else that might have slowed a person down. I found myself scrambling over the wreckage of people's homes, working around wrecked cars and trucks, and avoiding bodies. In one place, a car with four people inside had been thrown through an apartment building.

I was a couple of blocks from Lincoln park when I heard a noise behind me. I turned to see the demon, about a hundred yards behind me, but definitely heading my way. The Master had stopped it, and the monster had retreated.

I checked my shield, then took shelter in a half-demolished building. I had my spelled sword but little confidence that it would hurt the demon.

But I was shielded, and being young and dumb, decided to take a swing at it. As the demon passed me, it seemed to be smaller than I remembered. I leapt out of my hiding place and swung my sword at the back of its ankle. The sword bit deep into what in a human would be the Achilles tendon.

A shock traveled through the sword, up my arms, and into my shoulders. It was like I had taken a swing at a brick building. My sword glowed red with heat. The demon cried out and grabbed at the back of its leg, then swung around toward me.

Flame blasted into the demon from my right. Like from a flamethrower, but the flame was larger, engulfing the entire monster.

Standing in the middle of the street, both hands reaching out toward the demon, was Jodi. The flame was coming from her, and it didn't stop. I had seen a pyromancer throw fireballs before, but the volume and force of what she was bathing the demon in was like a blast furnace.

The demon stood there, gaping at her. She wasn't much taller than its knee. Then, it turned away from her and backhanded me into the wall behind me.

My shield took the brunt of the blow, but I felt as though every joint in my body had sprung. I struggled to stand, and managed it on the third try, my back braced against the wall.

The demon had moved on down the street.

Jodi appeared beside me.

"Katy! Katy? Are you all right?" She tried to touch me, but my shield prevented it.

"Yeah, I think so."

"Thank God! I thought you were dead!"

Shoving myself away from the wall, I staggered down the street after the demon. I wasn't in the mood to get within hitting distance of it again, so I tapped the ley line. Pulling every blue thread, rope, and ribbon, I sent them after it, wrapping it in blue water magic.

The result was similar to what Master Greenwood had done. The demon cried out and started to steam. I kept layering the threads around it until suddenly it leaped into the air.

It came down on the roof of a three-story building and disappeared from sight.

We continued until we hit the cross street, then took the trail where the demon had dropped back to the ground.

CHAPTER 31

We followed the demon to Lincoln Park. A block or so before we got there, we intersected the demon's trail from earlier that morning. It was going back to where it was summoned, the first time that it was doing that, to my knowledge.

The demon awaited us in a copse of trees behind the softball field. That was the place where the summoning ritual had been held as well. No one else was around, which was a disappointment to me and, evidently, to the demon. It was looking around, as though lost and unsure as to what to do next.

Pulling blue ribbons from the ley line, I began wrapping them around the demon, and it began steaming. And then it disappeared.

"Quick! Which bus stop is near here?" I asked.

"On 13th street, one block west, and one across the street," Jodi replied. She took a few steps closer to the summoning circle before I could stop her.

"Oh, my God!" She stumbled away and threw up. I was trying not to look at the girl in the circle. I glanced at her face, and she looked somewhat familiar. I followed Jodi and gathered her hair in my hands.

"Yeah, it's pretty bad," I said. "You've seen the demon. That is the sacrifice the summoner makes to bring it to this plane."

She stopped heaving, and I gave her a bottle of water from my bag to wash her mouth with.

"We have to hurry," I said. "When is the next bus?"

That gave her something to think about instead of the horror in the circle behind us.

"We've got about seven minutes, if it's on time."

Pulling on Jodi's arm, I got her moving, and we cleared the grove of trees. I picked up the summoner's trail, which was very fresh, and followed it out of the park and across the street to a bus stop going east. I could see the back end of a bus receding from us.

"It's here," I said. "The trail stops here."

Jodi nodded.

I called Dierdre while we waited and told her where the summoning site was located.

"Are you there now?" she asked.

"No, we're at a bus stop. We're going to try and follow the summoner."

"Keep in touch, okay?"

We caught the next bus, and drove the bus driver crazy, having him stop at each stop on his route so I could get off and search for the summoner's scent. But we struck gold at the public library's central repository. I motioned to Jodi, and she jumped off the bus to join me.

"Headed this way," I said, taking off north on a footpath between the library and the art museum. I followed the scent into Civic Center Park, then east across the park to Broadway. From there, we went back south, and then crossed at the light to the east.

"I know he's doing his best to confuse a tracker," I said.

"Lots of bus stops here near the Capitol," Jodi said. "The question is whether he takes another one to lose us, or takes one to his destination."

The scent ended at a stop where at least six routes converged.

Jodi shook her head. "Too many variables. I could take a bus from here to almost anywhere." So I called Dierdre and told her we had lost the trail.

"I have an idea," Jodi said when I hung up. "Can you get a few more trackers to help us?"

"At least one, maybe two. Possibly more. Why?"

"The next time the demon manifests, we could take some trackers to the ritual site, then drive them here. Wait for the summoner, instead of following him. I'll bet he's using this stop to muddle his trail. It's perfect."

"Aren't there other stops that would serve the same purpose?" I asked.

"Yeah, but this one is basically in the center of the ritual sites I have marked on our map."

I thought about it. I could get Loretta, and Morgan, if he was still in town. I wasn't sure, though, if all trackers had the ability to follow a magical scent the way I did. But the fact that the mage knew so much about trackers, and how to throw them off a trail was a puzzle. Most of the public knew nothing about trackers, or the Guild's bounty program.

We took a bus that dropped us off at Carlisle Square. It was past noon, and I was getting hungry. I knew Jodi's stomach was empty.

Master Rathske was standing near the cafeteria when we came into the Guild Hall.

"Ah, Kaitlyn," he called.

I could have pretended not to hear him, but I didn't think being rude to him was a good idea. He was a master, and I was only an apprentice.

"Yes, sir?"

"Were you out at the demon manifestation this morning?"

"Uh, yeah, I was there. Pretty ugly and a lot of damage west of Speer Boulevard."

"I understand that the Greenwoods engaged the demon."

"Yes. I really didn't see much of that, but Master Greenwood tried to drown it by diverting the creek."

He seemed to study my face, then looked thoughtful. "Interesting. Yes, they have indicated that they thought it was a fire demon, the same that manifested before."

"Yes, it looked like the same demon as I saw on Colfax that time," I said.

"But the water didn't work?"

"Made it turn around."

He nodded. "So, you weren't close to it today?"

"Well, later, after it turned around. It went back to Lincoln Park by the same way as it came this way."

"Like it couldn't change direction," Jodi said. "It was told to come east, and when it couldn't do that, it didn't know what to do."

That brought a raised eyebrow. "Now, that is interesting. You think someone, or something, is telling it what to do?"

"The summoner," Jodi said.

"You think it's being summoned? Not that it's manifesting on its own?"

"I've seen the ritual sites," I said. "That's where the demon returned to today, and then it vanished."

He leaned closer. "And was there a sacrifice associated with this site?"

"Yes, sir. A young girl was killed."

"Most unfortunate."

"I'm sure she thought so. Uh, we need to get something to eat. It's been a long time since breakfast."

"Oh, of course. Young girls need their nourishment."

I could feel his eyes on us all the way into the cafeteria.

"He is so creepy," Jodi said as we sat down with our meals.

"Yeah. He's been trying to get me to let him 'mentor' me since my parents died. I keep dodging him, hoping I'll grow out of his preferred age range."

"I like Master Greenwood much better."

I winked at her. "That just shows you have taste."

She nodded. "And a sense of self preservation."

CHAPTER 32

Marlene found us in the cafeteria. "There you are. Dierdre and the Master are asking for you. She's tried calling you, but all calls have been going straight to your voicemail. As soon as you finish, come up to my office."

"I've been busy," I said. She gave me an exasperated look. I didn't bother to explain that when I was tracking, I ignored outside distractions. It was too easy to lose the scent.

We were mostly finished with our meals, so we picked up and followed her. Once we were in her office, she punched a key on her desk phone and sat down behind her computer.

"Did you find them?" Dierdre's voice came from the speaker.

"They're with me now."

"Kaitlyn? Any luck?"

I gave her a brief account of our journey across town. "Did you find the ritual site in Lincoln Park?" I asked.

"Yes. The police have identified the sacrifice as Monica Ellis, age sixteen. They had her in their system as a runaway from a small town on the eastern plains. Did you know her?"

I looked at Jodi, who shook her head.

"I thought she looked familiar," I said, "but the name doesn't ring a bell. I can ask around the street kids." A thought struck me. "Can you tell if she'd been raped? Or any of the other victims?"

"The young girl, Simone, that you knew. None of the other women as far as the medical examiner could tell. We'll have to wait for the post-mortem to tell with this girl. Why?"

"Just a thought. DNA?"

"Yes. If we catch him, we'll be able to tie him to Simone's murder."

It was a risk, but I said, "So, the DNA you found isn't in the cops' database? How about the Guild's database?"

Silence for a few moments, then, "Not in the police database, which is national. We haven't run it against our database. But that is only local."

"So are the demon summonings."

Another bit of silence. "True. Marlene, do you have the accesses to do that?"

"Nope. I'm only an apprentice."

"Okay, I'll do it when I get back to the office." Dierdre said goodbye and hung up.

Marlene looked up at me. "You think one of our mages is doing this?"

I shrugged. "As they say on the TV cop shows, we can't rule it out until we check it, right?"

I sent Jodi home. Delia would be concerned that she hadn't come home the previous night, and I saw no reason for her to continue her bus route mappings. I went to my room to take a shower and change clothes. The slog through all the debris of the demon's destruction—as well as the encounter with him— had left a less than pleasant smell on me.

My intercom squawked, and Dierdre's voice said, "Kaitlyn? Can you come to my office?"

I hurried down there and found Dierdre alone.

"Close the door," she said after beckoning me in. She motioned to the chair in front of her desk and I sat.

"It turns out, that I don't have access to the Guild's DNA database, and when I asked my father about it, he told me that Master Olinsky has restricted that to the Council. He also said that she has denied use of it to search for our summoner."

"Which makes me more suspicious than ever," I said.

"Yes, but you and I aren't allowed to speculate about such suspicions. Do you understand me?"

"There's a coverup."

"Perhaps. And perhaps there are other issues we don't know about or understand."

"What would happen if an earth mage triggered an earthquake here, inside the wards?"

Dierdre looked startled. "Why, I'm not sure. I don't think it would be good." She seemed to think about it for a moment, then said, "It would probably be suicidal."

She sat back in her chair and studied me. "What are you thinking?"

"The summoner seems to understand a lot about trackers and our abilities. An earth mage who also has intimate knowledge of trackers has a thing for very young girls."

She sighed. "I'll mention this to my father, but I don't want you breathing a word of it to anyone. Anyone. Understand?"

I nodded. "Yes, ma'am."

Leaning forward, Dierdre said, "Right now, the Guild is walking on eggshells with the state and local authorities. And honey, you have no protection other than my father. Do not give Master Olinsky any excuse to use you as any kind of scapegoat. Now, get out of here and go see Marlene. She has lessons for you."

When I finished with Marlene, I wanted nothing more than to get out of the Guild Hall. My conversation with Dierdre had been eating away at me all afternoon. I decided that I would get dinner at Two Fools, then drop by the Tracker's Lounge to hear the gossip, and spend the night at my apartment at Mrs. O'Reilly's.

My fish and chips and second mug of ale had just been delivered to my table when a woman coming through the front door caught my attention. Other than her white-blonde hair, she wasn't particularly noticeable, but I had seen her only a short time before on Carlisle Square. When I left the Guild Hall, she was sitting on the steps of one of the banks nearby.

The hostess seated her at a table near me, and I watched her out of the corner of my eye. As far as I could tell, she wasn't watching me or paying any attention to me at all. I decided that the two of us being in the same place was just a coincidence.

I still took precautions when I left the pub. I cast a glamor on myself, and took a round-about way to the Tracker Lounge. As I pushed through the outer door, I exchanged that glamor for the one I always used in that bar.

As I expected, the place was packed, and the only seat I could find was at the bar. I ordered ale, and sat back to watch and listen. Some of the rumors were enough to make me laugh.

"So, what do you think about all this?" the bartender asked me.

"Pretty inventive, although the real thing was exciting enough."

"You saw the demon?"

"Yes. I was there when it crossed the bridge at 13th and Speer. It's the second time I've seen it."

"Fire demon from what I hear," he said.

"I think so. A fire mage tried to stop it and didn't have any luck. A water mage stopped it at the bridge and made it turn around. Seemed not to like the water."

He nodded. "I hadn't heard about a fire mage."

I grinned. "There's a place, a couple of blocks from Lincoln

Park, where the whole street is black and charred. That's where the fire mage and the fire demon had a little discussion."

He raised his eyebrows. "That's quite a ways from Speer and 13th."

I shrugged. "I'm a tracker. I was interested in where it was going."

A hand laid on my shoulder made me turn. Loretta leaned close and said into my ear, "Let's go someplace quieter, where we can talk."

Her car was parked outside, and we drove to a neighborhood bar a few blocks away. Other than the jukebox playing heartbroken-cowboy music, the place was as quiet as a tomb. I counted only fifteen people, including the bartender and a waitress.

We took a booth, and the waitress came to take our orders.

I told Loretta about my morning, leaving out the part about Jodi trying to incinerate a fire demon. I figured the fewer people who knew about Jodi, the better.

"I'm sure we almost caught up to the summoner," I told her. "He must have been only a couple of minutes ahead of me. My friend suggested that if we could get several trackers together, have them pick up the scent at the ritual site, and then drive them to that bus stop on Broadway, we might be able to identify him when he showed up there."

"Tricky on timing, and aren't there other bus stops he could use the same way?"

"Yeah. But if you take all the ritual sites we've found, that bus stop is in the center of their circle. I'm open to suggestions, though. This is getting out of hand."

"And the other stuff? The winds, the earthquakes?"

I shook my head. "I have no idea. Could it be the same person? Seems doubtful. Master Greenwood thinks it's more than one person."

CHAPTER 33

Loretta had an idea that probably never would occur to a mage from the Guild.

"I know a witch, a seer. I think we should consult her."

I took a deep breath and thought about it. "Really a seer? Magic, and not a con with a deck of Tarot cards?"

"Genuine. Doesn't hurt to go talk with her, does it?"

We agreed to meet for breakfast at a coffee shop near the witch's home the following morning.

When I got there, Loretta was waiting for me. But no sooner had I sat down and started to search the menu when the woman I had seen twice the day before walked in and took a booth near the entrance. She could see us easily, but we would have to turn conspicuously to see her.

"That woman who just walked in?" I said. "I have never seen her until yesterday, and now this is the third time. She has magic. I can tell. Do you know who she is?"

"I don't know who she is, but I know *what* she is."

I turned and looked, tapping the ley line. Her aura was very similar to Loretta's—a foggy gray, but with a white border.

Turning to face Loretta, I asked, "And what is she? Not an elemental mage."

Shaking her head, Loretta avoided the question by gesturing the waitress over.

"We're ready to order."

After the waitress left, I took a sip of my coffee and said, "C'mon, partner. Educate the young girl."

She obviously was debating with herself as to answering my question. Finally, she said, "She's a kind of daywalker."

"She has magic," I said. "That would mean her mother was a mage."

"Or a witch." It dawned on me what the two women's auras conveyed, and the reason behind their differences. Loretta was a dhampir whose mother was a witch. The other woman's mother was probably a mage. That was why I could feel her magic. It was familiar to me, whereas Loretta's was not.

We ate our breakfast, paid, and left, then sat in Loretta's car in the parking lot for half an hour, but the blonde didn't come out.

"It doesn't seem that she's stalking you," Loretta said.

"No. It's kinda weird seeing her three times in two days, but I would know if someone was following me. I guess it's just her hair that makes her noticeable."

"Could be." She started the car, and we drove over to the witch's house for our ten o'clock appointment.

The witch, Adelheid Bauer, was straight out of central casting. Her house was a perfect white clapboard cottage, complete with picket fence. Roses and other flowers filled the front yard.

Inside, it looked like a Goth teenager's wet dream. The walls were painted black, and the paintings hanging there looked like a celebration of Halloween, including demons. At least three different black cats came to investigate our intrusion.

And then there was Adelheid. Gray hair that looked as

though she'd lost her hairbrush, and a black mourning dress circa 1853. Her complexion was pale, her nose was slightly crooked down, and she had a large mole on the left side of her chin. But what caught you were her eyes—so dark that the irises were almost black.

A tea service with cookies sat on a low table in the middle of the living room. Adelheid indicated that we should sit, and flounced down in a large overstuffed chair.

"How is your grandmother doing?" she asked Loretta without preamble, and I thought I caught a tiny bit of a German accent.

"Fine, although getting a bit creaky and cranky. She's almost a hundred."

"Well, if that's the worst you tell her about me, I'll take it. What can I do for you?"

She leaned forward and poured three cups of tea as Loretta spoke.

"You know about the demon that's been terrorizing the city. We're trying to find the summoner."

Adelheid put the teapot down and looked up.

"And you need a seer because you're not having any luck."

"Yes, ma'am," I responded.

For the first time, she really paid attention to me, looking me up and down. She seemed to spend a long time gazing at something over my head.

"Do you care about the difference between right and wrong, good and evil, order and chaos?" she finally said.

"Yes, ma'am."

"And where do you fall?"

I shifted uneasily in my chair, then said, "I'm more comfortable with good over evil and order over chaos. Is that what you mean?" I didn't want to get into a discussion of right and wrong with anyone. Those concepts were so flexible. But I had seen evil, knew it was real, and wanted no part of it.

She nodded, then looked toward Loretta. "Damned good for all of us. You don't know what you have, but she's special."

Picking up her teacup and taking a sip, she leaned back in her chair. "Talk to me. Tell me what you know about this summoner. Do you know where she's holding her rituals? Have you seen where she's placing her alter?"

I told her about the summoning sites and the ritual layouts, including the sacrifices. "Why are you using 'she' and 'her'?" I asked. "What makes you think it's a woman?"

Adelheid shrugged. "Nothing in particular. It could be a hermaphrodite or a man. I just like feminine pronouns. Now, I'll need to see one of these sites. Preferably when it's still fresh. The smell of brimstone probably masks the scent of the summoner's magic, but it will be strongest immediately after the ritual is completed."

I nodded. "That's true, but the scent of magic can still be detected at least a week later."

The old woman's eyebrows lifted. It was the first sign of emotion I had seen.

"*You* can detect it a week later?"

"Yes, ma'am."

She turned her attention to Loretta. "And *you*?"

Loretta shook her head. "I've seen only one ritual site, and it was old. Katy has seen several, including one where the mage was still near."

"That site is just a couple of days old," I said, "but it's been cleaned up."

Adelheid nodded, put down her teacup, and stood. "Take me there."

We all piled into Loretta's pickup and drove to Lincoln Park. To my dismay, the ritual site had really been cleaned up. The chalk circles were gone, as was the blood from the poor girl we had found there.

The brimstone stink was still there, though, and I could faintly feel the magic of the summoner.

Adelheid walked around, studying the ground. Even though no markings were visible, I noted that she never stepped on or over where they had been.

"You say the lines were drawn with chalk?" she asked.

"Chalk laced with salt. And then the victim's blood was dribbled onto the lines."

She peered around some more, then said, "If you can take me to a site that is new, and undisturbed, then I can probably read the person who is doing this. You're sure it's always the same demon?"

"Unless he has a twin."

Adelheid chuckled. "Tweedle-dee and Tweedle-dum. I don't think that's likely."

CHAPTER 34

I hadn't been home in a while, and always felt a little uneasy when I didn't check on the place regularly. Loretta and I had lunch at Two Fools, then I told her I had some errands to run.

The apartment turned out to be fine. Nothing out of place, and the heat was still on low as I'd left it. The water lines were intact. I stopped by Mrs. O'Reilly's apartment, and she handed me a stack of junk mail. I couldn't figure out how anyone got my address, since I hardly used it for anything. I sorted it next to the garbage cans outside, keeping only one letter from the licensing bureau telling me that I needed to renew my PI license.

Thinking about dinner, I decided to grab a free steak at the Guild Hall, and wandered in that direction, not in any hurry.

The changes in my life over the past few weeks gave me a lot to ponder about. There were new people, new sources of income, new educational opportunities, and new dangers. A lot to take in, and it felt as though I had been swept along without a chance to catch my breath. Compared to when I was desperate enough to track Madeleine du Mont, I almost felt like a different person.

I couldn't really identify any decisions I'd made that were uncomfortable. Not in a right-or-wrong sort of way. Uncomfortable in stretching me, taking me out of my comfort zone, yes. But nothing I regretted or that made me feel guilty.

Even being swallowed by the Guild didn't feel constricting, and that surprised me. In some ways, it kinda felt like I was accepting Master Greenwood as a father figure, and Dierdre, if not a mother figure, then at least as the older sister I'd never had. Marlene was Marlene. I guessed that even in biological families a person probably felt closer to some people than to others.

The sun was setting as I passed through a neighborhood known for vampires. Some of the local vamps were quite wealthy, and had bought up a couple of blocks of apartment buildings, bricked up all the windows, and rented them to their undead brethren. During the day, the area was as safe as Sunday School, and since most vamps were law-abiding, not too bad at night. There were several nightclubs in the vicinity—owned and run by the aforementioned wealthy vamps—that had a heavy college student clientele.

Everyone had their own kinks, and as long as people left me alone, I didn't pass judgement on others' lifestyles. But it seemed to me that it was easy enough to get laid without worrying about severe anemia for weeks afterward. Although with a vamp lover, a human didn't have to worry about diseases or pregnancy—with one very major exception.

Passing by an alley a couple of blocks from the nearest meat-market club, I heard a rustling. Out of habit, I cast my shield just as two vamps jumped out of the shadows. They seemed surprised to find that they couldn't grab me.

"Wrong girl," I said, drawing my sword with one hand, and

pulling a stake from my bag with the other. "Now, why don't you run along home and we can avoid any unpleasantness?"

To my surprise, they were joined by three more vamps coming at me from behind. I decided that it was probably a little too late for negotiating, so I feinted at the vamp on my right with the stake, and took his head with the sword.

Whirling around, I met another vamp with the stake. He took it too high in the chest, so I didn't nail his heart. I pushed him away and kicked him in the stomach. A vamp came from my left, and I slashed at him, but he jumped out of the way. Something heavy slammed into my back, like the kick of a mule, knocking me forward, but I managed to keep my feet.

The vamp on my left jumped on me, bearing me to the ground. One thing my dad and Scott had always harped on was, if you were on the ground in a fight, you were toast. I reached out to the ley line and indiscriminately pulled the threads of magic to me.

A burst of white light turned the night into more than day. The vamp no longer held me down, and I struggled to my feet. Five vamps lay still within twenty feet of me, and one was crawling away. Down the alley, I saw the back of someone running. He turned the corner out of sight, and I returned my attention to the vamp trying to make her getaway.

I walked up behind her, and set the point of my sword in front of her face. She stopped crawling.

"Just as a matter of curiosity," I said, "why did you decide to attack me?" With the way my heart was hammering, I was rather surprised at how calm I sounded.

She didn't answer, but tried to crawl around the sword. I leaned forward and placed my other stake on her back. She stopped and shuddered. It was dark, and my night sight was no better than most humans, but it appeared that her face had a stunned expression.

"I can wait," I said, crouching down and moving the sword

so that the blade sat on the back of her neck. Most female vamps are turned young, but she looked about forty. She could have been turned the week before, or during the Roman Empire.

"We were hired," she rasped.

"Oh? By whom? And to attack me, or just any random human?"

"You."

I pressed on the stake, the point penetrating the fabric of her dress. "And?"

"A mage. I don't know his name."

"Was he here? The guy who ran away?"

"Probably. Yeah."

"Describe him."

She tried to raise her head, and I could see some bit of awareness starting to dawn on her face.

"Tall, dark hair, beard. Please. Let me go."

I pushed the stake into her heart. No matter what she told me, there was a major chance that it was a lie. Vampires had no morals or ethics, and all they cared about was their own survival.

Another puzzle to solve, or was it part of the same puzzle? The mage was an aeromancer, of that I was sure. I had seen the color of the magic he wielded. As to what I had done with the ley line, I was completely confused. All of the vamps were dead —final death—but some didn't have a mark on them.

I continued to the Guild Hall, but a lot more cautiously than before. When I reached there, I went immediately to Dierdre's office. Sure enough, she was there. The woman was a workaholic.

"Hi Kaitlyn," she said with a smile. "What's up?"

"Have you had any dinner?"

She glanced at the clock on her desk.

"As a matter of fact, no."

"Neither have I. Can you give me twenty minutes to wash the vampire blood off me, and meet me in the dining room? I just got ambushed, and want to talk about it."

"Sure. Are you okay?"

"I think so. Can an aeromancer destroy a person's shield?"

"Possibly, depending on the relative strength of the two mages."

"I guess I was stronger. See you in twenty."

The dark-maroon vampire blood didn't look as though it would wash out of my shirt. I stuck it in the sink with cold water and some soap, but when I came out of the shower, the water was still clear. Another reason to avoid confrontations with vampires.

I started to pull a clean shirt and new slacks from my closet, but hesitated. After rolling around a dirty alley in vampire blood, I had a sudden urge to feel girlie.

I went to the closet and pulled one of the two dresses I had bought with my new-found wealth. It was a burgundy V-neck long-sleeve midi that had captured my attention when I saw it in a shop window. It was meant for a shorter girl than me, so the hem fell only a couple of inches below my knees, but I was skinny enough to wear the petite size. The V-neck would have shown off my cleavage to advantage, if I had any. Shoes were another matter, but I had a new pair of black calf-high boots with flat heels that turned out to look good with the dress.

I stared at my reflection in the mirror. I hadn't worn a dress in more than two years. When I had seen Dierdre in her office, she was wearing a nice blouse and a skirt. So, for a change, I wanted to look like someone she might want to have dinner with instead of a street urchin.

She was waiting for me at a table for two along one wall. I crossed the room and noted that I wasn't being watched by everyone. There were some men who looked, but it was with approval rather than distaste.

"You look very nice," Dierdre said when I sat down. "That's new, isn't it?"

My cheeks burned. "Yes. First time I've worn it."

She motioned to the menu. "Do you know what you want?"

"Yes. Do you know how to get vamp blood out of a shirt?"

With a wink, she said, "Magic. We'll see if you're able to do it yourself, or if you have to send it to the laundry. What's this about being ambushed? Vampires and aeromancers?"

The waiter came over, and I ordered a steak with a fancy potato, and Dierdre helped me choose a glass of wine.

"I was just walking through that vamp neighborhood over on 19th west of downtown, and six vampires jumped me. There was an aeromancer with them, but I didn't get a good look at him. One of the vamps told me he had paid them to attack me. She didn't know why, and she didn't know his name."

"None of them survived?"

I shook my head. "I did something with the ley line. Dierdre, I killed them with magic, but I don't know how. And then the mage ran."

"Take it slow, and try and tell me exactly what you did."

I thought back. "He was hammering me. I guess with some kind of air magic. Like with a sledge hammer smashing against my shield. Then one of the vamps jumped on my back and knocked me off my feet. I guess I panicked. I reached for the ley line and pulled magic from it—every color of thread. There was a blast of white light, and all the vamps were dead. Except one. She was farthest from me, but she was stunned and couldn't stand. The mage ran away down an alley."

"Dear Goddess."

"Dierdre, what do you see when you look at my aura? I can't see it in a mirror."

"No, auras don't show that way. Kaitlyn, your aura is like watching the most vivid rainbow you can imagine. Constantly changing, rippling with every color—hell, with some colors I don't even have a name for. We think you're a spirit mage. You know that spirit is the fifth element, right? But we don't have any spirit mages here in Queen City. It's the rarest kind of elemental magic. I've read about it, and I can give you stuff to read. But I don't know what you did. We'll have to talk to Father."

I chuckled. "Do babies have auras?"

"Oh, yes, very bright ones!"

"My middle name is Iris, which is associated with rainbows in Ireland."

"And your father was Irish, right?"

I nodded. "That's one of the reasons my grandparents hated him. They're descended from English aristocracy, and consider the Irish savages."

The waiter brought our wine, and I took a sip. It tasted like cherries.

"But the question is, why would someone pay a bunch of vamps to attack me? It has to be tied to me trying to track the summoner. Hell, unless there's been some sort of general announcement I wasn't privy to, almost no one knows I'm here. Or why."

CHAPTER 35

After dinner, Dierdre drove me out to her father's estate. She parked around the back and used the door into the kitchen. I felt like a burglar, but reminded myself that she grew up in that huge mansion. I did feel the ward as we passed through it, and knew that she had done something to allow us entry.

We found Master Greenwood in what appeared to be either a library or a study—or maybe both. My knowledge of mansions was primarily limited to what I saw in books or on TV. It was paneled in golden-brown wood, and there was a fire burning in the fireplace. The Master sat in a chair by the fire, and he laid a book on the table beside him when we came in.

"To what do I owe this pleasant surprise?" he asked with a smile. "Very pretty, Kaitlyn. Did anyone ever tell you—"

"That I look like my mother when she was sixteen? I think it's been mentioned a few times."

He roared with laughter, then sobered, and said, "Come in, come in. What can I get you? Tea, or a cordial, perhaps? Dierdre, there are some of those green-frosted little cookies you like in the kitchen. Mrs. Brown just baked them today."

I sat, but Dierdre turned and left the room, tossing her coat on a small couch on her way out.

"So, what's the occasion?" he asked, looking me up and down.

"Uh, we had dinner in the dining room. I, uh, I guess I just wanted to look nice so that people didn't frown at me. It gets kinda uncomfortable sometimes."

He nodded. "Camouflage. I usually wear a business suit when I go downtown. Wizard robes stand out a little too much at the State Capitol."

I mentally pictured him wearing something out of the "Sorcerer's Apprentice" and delivering a speech to the legislature. It made me smile.

The Master smiled back. "Well, that's a better expression than the one you wore when you came in here. What's the problem?"

Dierdre came back with the cookies and some herbal tea, and poured me a cup while I told the Master about the ambush.

When I finished, he said, "An aeromancer. You know, even a very strong shield will hold up to most magic, but you can get very hot fighting a pyromancer, and an aeromancer can cast a shield outside of yours that is air tight. Lack of oxygen is a pretty nasty weapon. Have you ever put your hand in front of a heavy air gun? That sounds like the kind of blasts he was aiming at you."

"Yeah, I figured that. But what did *I* do?"

"You know what happens when you shine sunlight through a prism?" he asked. "You did the opposite. But magic doesn't like being compressed like that, so it escaped. That escape took the form of an explosion. It's not something I would encourage you to do again, or to try and practice using it as a weapon—at least not in the city. Maybe out at the Farm. But if you're ever captured by a dragon and held in its castle miles from nowhere, it might be a way out."

The twinkle in his eye told me he was teasing me. My dad used to look that way sometimes when he was pulling my leg.

"First you want me to track demons, and now dragons. I want a raise."

Both the Master and Dierdre laughed.

"What worries me is the ambush," I said. "A mage paid vamps to kill me? I never heard of such a thing."

The Master shifted in his seat. His expression had gone from humorous to uncomfortable. I glanced at Dierdre, and she was staring expectantly at her father.

"Well, it would lend some credence to the theory of some disgruntled mages being responsible for all these troubles," he said.

"When I first heard about the demon, there were rumors that it had killed some mages—that it was directed at the Guild. But that's not what it's been doing."

He shook his head. "Master Olinsky was meeting with the Mayor at City Hall. If you trace the demon's path, that could be where it was heading."

"Okay, but why take me out? If I was sniffing around close to the summoner, I could see it. But so far, we don't have a clue."

"Dad, tell her," Dierdre said. "She should know."

He looked hard at his daughter, then gave a big sigh.

"Kaitlyn, when your parents died, did you ever wonder about how a pair of vampires were able to kill both of them? Your dad was a top tracker, with many of the same talents that you have, and your mom was a strong Guild-certified mage."

"Yeah. It's always been a puzzle. But the Guild posted bounties on those two vamps."

"And you hunted them down and took them out. A fourteen-year-old girl. Yes, they might have been directly responsible for your parents' deaths. But there was evidence that they had magical help. The trap your dad walked into kept him from invoking his shield. And I personally think it took more than two vampires to defeat him. We think your mom confronted the mage directly and lost a battle to him or her. The bounties were posted quietly, and I've always considered those two vampires scapegoats."

My head was spinning. "And why hasn't anyone ever told me this?"

"You were too young to confront a mage your mother couldn't beat—even if you could track them down. Trust me, we were shocked when we discovered that you showed up to claim the bounties. What bothers me about your story tonight is the mage involvement. And if the two incidents are linked, then you really need to watch your step."

"I didn't know you could stop a mage from casting their shield. Why do you think the Guild was shocked about me claiming the bounties? When did you find out about that?"

"Just recently, after Madeleine du Mont. I was shocked. Master Rathske seemed to know about you, but I assure you that no one on the Council was even aware of your existence."

"We're really not certain how you fell through the cracks," Dierdre said. "Master Olinsky is not happy about that. And you've been collecting bounties for years. A minor. Tonight, you defeated six vampires and a mage. Sixteen-year-old girls aren't supposed to be doing things like that."

I wanted to say that sixteen—hell, fourteen-year-old—girls are supposed to be protected by adults. But instead, I said, "Master Rathske has known me all along. He personally paid me the bounties for the vamps that killed my parents. Believe me, there isn't a fourteen-year-old girl who ever walked into the Guild Hall that he doesn't know about. He's already offered to mentor Jodi."

Master Greenwood's eyes widened, and he turned to Dierdre.

"He does like his women young," Dierdre said. "I didn't know he liked them quite that young."

"Did he ever hit on you?" the Master asked.

"Oh, yeah, but I think I was sixteen the first time." She said it offhandedly.

The expression on the Master's face showed surprise, and then possibly anger. His jaw muscles worked, and it seemed like he wanted to say something. Instead, he looked away from us. I thought it was kind of funny that he wasn't aware of our reality. I got hit on almost every day. I couldn't imagine what it was like to be as beautiful as Dierdre or Jodi.

"Did you get DNA results for the most recent girl?" I asked.

Dierdre shook her head. "Not yet."

"Have you checked the results from Simone's autopsy against the Guild's database?"

"Most of the older mages—and I don't think any of the masters—aren't in that database," Master Greenwood said. "But I will speak with Master Olinsky, and see what we do have."

On our way back to the Guild, Dierdre said, "You really need a necklace to go with that dress. And some different shoes. We'll have to go shopping."

"Oh, I have jewelry, but not in my room at the Guild. I might have been young and naïve when the bank kicked me out, but not stupid. I took all my mom's jewelry with me." It was all stashed in the safe at Scott's dojo, along with most of my bounty money from Madeleine.

"Well, you need some decent shoes, and your hair needs trimming. First thing tomorrow."

CHAPTER 36

The following morning, Dierdre came to my room and checked out all the clothes I had in my closet. Then it took about fifteen minutes for her to show me how to separate cloth from vampire blood. I couldn't believe it was so easy.

Afterwards, she bundled me into her car and took me to a store I never would have considered if left to my own devices. I thought we were going to buy a couple dresses, but I discovered she wanted to buy me an entire wardrobe. Then I had to argue with her for two hours over what kind of shoes I needed.

"No! Absolutely not! I will either break my neck or my ankle. Read my lips. No high heels! Hell, I don't need to be any taller." I couldn't figure out why Dierdre and Diana Olinsky wore heels. Both were over six feet. Maybe some kind of dominance game.

I ended up with five pairs of women's shoes, two of which had two-inch block heels. It was a compromise, but I took it as a win. I didn't have to wear them. I also had three new dresses, four skirts, four pairs of trousers, and eight blouses. It was getting closer to summer, and I thought t-shirts would be a good idea, but that didn't happen.

When I protested about the expense, Dierdre said, "This is all a gift from Father. Now, shut up."

The next stop was in a salon next door. As the hairdresser was finishing with me, Dierdre got a call.

"When we get back to the Hall," she said on our way back to the car, "change, and meet me in the dining room. Dad said that Master Olinsky invited us to lunch."

Just what I wanted to hear. More than two years doing my damnedest to fly under the radar, and suddenly everyone wanted a piece of me.

She parked the car in the garage and helped me carry stuff to the elevator.

"Wear the dark-blue skirt and a white blouse," she said. "And the black shoes with heels."

Dierdre got off on the first floor, and I proceeded on to the seventh. I managed to balance all the shoe boxes and the clothes until I got to my room, then just dropped the lot so I could open the door. I piled everything onto the bed, cut the tags off the clothing she told me to wear, put on a pair of pantyhose for the first time in years, ran a brush through my hair, and bounced out of the door.

Rushing into the dining room, I looked around but didn't see anyone I recognized. A waiter caught my eye and pointed toward a nook on the far side of the room. Around the table were Masters Greenwood and Olinsky, Dierdre, and an older man I didn't know.

Master Olinsky looked up as I approached, and motioned to a chair across from her.

"Hello, Kaitlyn. This is Master O'Hara. Liam, this is Kaitlyn Dunne, Lee and Sarah Dunne's daughter."

So, I was sitting across from the three top members of the Guild Council. The feeling of unreality that often hit me in the Guild Hall enveloped me. I was nervous before, but suddenly I was almost shaking. I did manage to pull out a chair next to Dierdre and sit in it without falling on my face.

A waiter showed up and stood looking at me. I was the only one with a menu in front of me. I ordered a salad that Dierdre often ordered for her lunch, the guy took the menu, and left.

"Tell us about this incident last night," Master Olinsky said.

So, I told the story again. When I finished, Master O'Hara leaned on his elbows and said, "I understand you're a tracker. Forgive me, but I didn't expect someone so young. I understand that you're the one who killed Madeleine du Mont?"

My cheeks suddenly felt very warm. "A girl has to eat. It pays better than waiting tables. And Madeleine drowned. She got careless."

The line between his eyebrows deepened. "But aren't you in school?"

"I-I, uh, I guess I dropped out." My face felt so hot I was afraid my hair would combust.

Master Olinsky patted his arm and said, "I'll tell you about it later. It's really not relevant to this discussion."

He nodded and was quiet for a bit, then asked, "You're sure it was a mage who attacked you?"

"An aeromancer. He couldn't break through my shield, though."

Master Olinsky said, "We had a complaint from the Vampire Council this morning, that a mage attacked and killed six of their members last night."

I couldn't help it, I burst out laughing. "Yeah, that's what I do for kicks at night. Because I'm so much faster and stronger than the average vamp, I go hunting them. I know that vamps have no sense of humor, but do they even understand how ridiculous that sounds?"

I saw the grave expression on Master O'Hara's face momentarily crack.

"There have been a few suggestions that some of our trackers are freelancing," Master Greenwood said.

Sometimes I let my emotions get ahead of my common sense. Freelancing? That pissed me off.

"And there are a bunch of bloodsuckers who are freelancing on the street people," I replied. "I can show you a thirteen-year-old girl who had her arm almost chewed off. And then someone's using kids as sacrifices to summon demons. There are a lot of new vamps roaming around downtown. Ask their council when those vamps who died last night were turned. And by whom. If they can't keep their own house in order, don't blame the trackers."

I realized that I'd been a little too hot, and everyone was staring at me.

"The real issue we need to deal with," Master Greenwood said, "is, why a mage is trying to kill one of our trackers? And is that mage registered with the Guild, or is he a rogue?"

"And this particular tracker is a Guild member," Dierdre said. "My student and apprentice, registered, and overseen by a master."

Two waiters brought our meals, and the conversation died out. A little later, the three masters all looked up, their gazes focused behind me. Then I heard the voice.

"Diana, I don't mean to interrupt, but this is the first time I've seen you in a while. Well, since that du Mont woman killed Gerald. Hope you're doing well."

"Thank you, Evelyn," Master Olinsky said. "Yes, I'm doing okay other than all this messy demon crap. This is the young woman who took care of the Madeleine du Mont problem."

Her eyes fell to me. I turned and looked up. "Hello, Grandmother."

I kind of knew what the word 'aghast' meant, but I almost wanted to laugh at the look on her face. She took a couple of stumbling steps backward, then whirled, and walked away.

Once, she glanced back over her shoulder, then continued even faster.

I turned back and met Master Olinsky's eyes. "She hasn't changed much in eight years," I said. "I guess I have. I'm a foot or so taller, for one thing." I went back to eating my salad.

After a while, everyone except me seemed to have a meeting of one sort or another to go to. The question of why a mage wanted me dead was never resolved, nor was any kind of concrete plan for solving the mystery decided upon. I felt a lot the way I did after my parents died. On my own in a sinking boat with a broken paddle.

I changed clothes and went over to Scott's dojo to take a little of my frustration out on the heavy bag.

CHAPTER 37

"What are you doing Saturday?" Scott asked.

"Nothing that I know about. Why?"

"Because there's a tournament here, and I think you need to test for your brown belt."

I stared at him. "Saturday? I have three days to prepare?"

Scott shrugged. "Have you been practicing? Come on, show me your forms."

He led me to a practice room and had me go through my forms. Three times. Then he waved to a guy, who came over. He was in his early twenties, a little taller than I was, but probably outweighed me by forty or fifty pounds. He was wearing a black belt.

The punch was unexpected, but I deflected it. The kick that followed it caught me on the leg. I went down, but rolled and came up behind him. He was fast, but much slower than the vampires and werewolves I was used to fighting. My punch to his kidney missed the mark as he turned, but it still landed in his side.

Ducking low, I swept one of his feet with my leg, knocking him off balance. My next move might not have been strictly standard. I rushed him, hitting him with my body, punching him in the stomach, grabbing his hair with my other hand, and knocking him off his feet. He bounced up, and his expression had changed from mildly amused to determined, and maybe a little pissed. He blocked my kick, and I blocked his punch. We settled down into a standard match with neither of us landing much of a blow and not wanting to get too close.

Scott called a halt, and my opponent and I bowed to each other.

"Not exactly standard form," Scott said.

"But effective," I countered.

He threw a punch at my head. I ducked and blocked it, moving away from him and assuming a defensive stance.

"I think you're ready for brown," he said. "But when you test, try to keep the street fighting to a minimum, okay? You'll be fighting multiple opponents in three-minute bouts. You don't have to destroy them, just keep even."

After spending two years feeling lucky to eat one meal a day, sometimes one meal every couple of days, being able to eat daily was a luxury. I was gaining weight, and had a lot more energy. Whatever reservations I had about the Guild were smothered by that kind of basic survival equation. I was sitting in a small café at lunch time when my phone rang.

"Kaitlyn!" Dierdre said the instant I answered. "The demon is rampaging through Capitol Hill. Where are you?"

I told her and said, "I can get there faster by bus than waiting on you to come get me."

I paid my tab and called Loretta on my way to the bus stop. "Can you get Mrs. Bauer and meet me at that bus stop on Broadway? The demon has appeared on Capitol Hill."

"On my way," she said.

I caught a bus that didn't require transfers to my destination, then I called Dierdre.

"I'm headed to the Broadway bus stop. Where is the demon?"

"It just crossed Speer at 13th."

The same path it had taken the last time.

"Is Master Olinsky meeting with the Mayor at city hall?" I asked.

A hesitation. "I don't know. I'll check."

The summoner had a tendency to repeat himself or herself. There had to be a reason besides laziness. If they were a chaos mage, that tendency would be random. Wouldn't it? I had so many random facts and suppositions, that trying to tie them into a coherent picture was daunting. If I were a deranged mage wanting to cause random chaos and destruction, what would I do? Without a motive, the questions became meaningless.

A grudge against the Guild? Hatred of humankind? Revenge against society? All of those sounded like a bad movie plot. The attack on me, and the revelations from Master Greenwood concerning my parents, led me to wonder if there was a personal motive. I could wrap my mind around that easier. For one thing, the chaos was localized in Queen City. Wouldn't some kind of master villain be more megamaniacal? If I wanted to create major chaos and take over the world, I'd be doing all the shit in Washington, not Queen City.

I called Dierdre.

"Where is the summoning site? What's the demon's path?"

"It's following the same path as last time. Lincoln Park maybe? No one has tried to figure it out yet, but it seems to be following the same route as last time."

"Then why isn't anyone at Lincoln Park? Gods, Dierdre. Do we have to be so reactive? Is anyone other than us doing anything besides trying to figure out who's to blame?"

She hung up. I called Loretta.

"Swing by that site at Lincoln Park. The summoner might have used the same ritual site."

"Will do."

By the time I reached the Broadway bus stop near the Capitol, I was so keyed up I was practically vibrating. I couldn't wait to get off the bus.

I scanned around, looking for Dierdre or her car. Moving through the crowd, I stopped when I saw the woman with white-blonde hair. She was standing on a rise just above the bus stop, staring down at me. There were other people around her, and for the first time I noticed how tall she was.

I guessed she was probably in her thirties, rather attractive, although dressed not to attract attention—jeans, a flannel shirt, work boots, all covered with a tan duster. She was wearing sunglasses, even though the day wasn't that bright.

I worked my way through the crowd and climbed up to where she had been. She was gone, but I could feel the traces of her magic. Were they the same as those of the summoner? I couldn't tell.

Looking around, I saw Dierdre's car parked against the curb on the cross street. She was standing next to the car waving at me. Walking down toward her, I called Loretta on my phone.

"What do you have?" I asked when Loretta answered.

"She has a rough feel for the summoner. Female. Adelheid thinks she isn't an elemental mage, but she's not sure. In any case, she's not particularly strong. Very good at ritual."

"That's not particularly useful," I said. "I saw the blonde dhampir at the Broadway bus stop. She disappeared, though. But wouldn't she fit the profile?"

"Yeah. I knew I shoulda taken the bitch out when I had the chance."

"There's something you're not telling me, partner."

"If you see her again, don't turn your back on her."

Loretta severed the connection as I reached Dierdre.

"Anything?" she asked.

"Not much. There's a dhampir we should look out for. Tall, white-blonde bob. She was here a couple of minutes ago, and she fits the profile of the summoner at Lincoln Park."

Dierdre said some words I thought her father would disapprove of, then, "Get in."

I jumped into the shotgun seat, and she squealed the tires getting out of there.

CHAPTER 38

"Where are we going?"
"Away from here. Around the northeast side of the Capitol. The demon is headed straight toward that bus stop."

I looked back. There were probably forty or fifty people there, either getting off a bus or waiting for one.

"What about all those people?"

"That's the cops' problem. Dad and Liam and Diana are gathered on the front steps of the Capitol. We'll ditch the car and join them."

"I don't think I'm going to be much help." I hoped she agreed. I did not want to confront that demon again. "Maybe you could drop me off in Boulder and come back." Boulder was the university town thirty miles north of Queen City.

She laughed. "Don't think that's not tempting. But you can tap the ley line and feed power to the mages. I'll show you how."

Olinsky was air and fire, Greenwood was water, and O'Hara was water and earth. Dierdre was air and water.

"Who else will be there?"

"As far as I know, just the five of us. The Council was meeting with the Mayor and the Governor when the demon appeared."

"At the same ritual site in Lincoln Park," I said, "and it's taking the same route as last time, but it's traveling a lot faster because it already cleared a path."

I pulled out my phone and updated Loretta. "Be careful," I said before I hung up. "In addition to the demon, there's going to be some crazy powerful magic flying around."

Dierdre parked the car, and we practically ran to the Capitol. Some police tried to stop us at one point, but Dierdre was shielded and just brushed them aside. I decided that was my cue to cast my own shield.

The Capitol sat on a low hill, and tiers of steps led from the park in front of the building up to the entrance. We found the masters gathered there, along with four other mages I didn't know. From that vantage point, we could see the demon.

Very quickly, Dierdre took me aside and said, "You can see everyone's auras, right?"

"Uh huh."

She spun some air magic, a tiny whirlwind on the ground in front of her. "And you can see what kind of magic I used to do that?"

"Yes. Air magic uses the white threads."

She slowly shook her head. "Gods, I have no idea what you see. Okay, now can you pull white threads from the ley line?"

"Sure."

"And push them into me?"

"Uh, are you sure that won't hurt you?"

"Feed them to me slowly."

I tried, and saw her light up. "Should I try with the blue ones, too?"

"The blue ones?"

"Yeah, water. You can use water, also, right?"

She nodded. I pulled a blue thread and pushed it toward her, and saw the halo of light around her turn sky blue. She looked startled, and said, "That is amazing. Most mages simply pull pure power and feed it to another mage. I've never seen anyone differentiate it like that."

"But you don't see the colors in the ley line, right?"

"No, I don't. You can see the auras of all the mages here? You can tell what their magic is?"

"Yeah, if they use magic, I can tell what kind of magic they're using. Dierdre, can I hurt anyone doing this?"

She shook her head. "Just make the magic available to them. Brush them with it, and let them take it."

"I'll try."

Dierdre went over to her father and whispered to him. He turned and looked at me. I brushed him with a blue thread, and saw him draw it in, then nod.

The demon had reached the bottom of the stairs and started up toward us. A small tornado appeared and slammed into it. Water, drawn out of the air, rained on it. The mages attacked with magic I didn't even know how to categorize, but I could see its colors, and pulled threads from the ley line to augment them.

The ground began to rumble and shake, then heave. The shaking made the earthquake at Carlisle Square look tame. I was knocked off my feet, as were the other mages. I could see the mage in the park who was casting the spell, but he was too far away to identify. I could just see the magic he was using.

The demon took advantage and leaped up the steps toward us. Master O'Hara stepped forward, casting earth magic to try and counteract the earthquake. The demon reached him, grabbed him, and swallowed him whole. Then the ground under the demon opened up, and it fell into the crevasse.

The earthquake and its aftershocks continued for several minutes. The mage who had cast it was gone, and I didn't see where he went. What I was sure of was that the flavor, the substance, of that mage was very different from that of the summoner. We were definitely fighting at least two people.

Master O'Hara was gone. I didn't even want to think about where. It had never occurred to me that the demon might be able to swallow me whole even though I was shielded. Was the master still inside the demon when it went back to its own plane of existence, or was he buried in the earth? I couldn't feel him.

The city was a mess. The Capitol was a mess. The demon had spared the art museum and the main library, but the earthquake had not. Dierdre and Master Greenwood and I made our way back to her car. The tree we had parked under had been uprooted, but it missed the car when it fell. The roads were a mess, and trying to drive through the debris, cracked streets, wrecked vehicles, and emergency personnel going every direction was crazy.

"Don't go to the Hall," Master Greenwood said. "Go out to the house. I don't think the damage will be too bad out there."

He was right. The quake's epicenter had been the Capitol. The effort, both of the demon and the geomancer, had been to take out the Council. We saw damage along our way, but less as we moved away from Capitol Hill. Dierdre avoided the major freeways, so it took us some time following surface streets.

"Who has a grudge against the Council?" I asked.

"How long a list do you want?" the Master asked.

"Maybe," Dierdre said, "but, Dad, Liam makes the fourth member of the Council to die in the past three months. I know that Madeleine was supposedly responsible for Gerald and Donita, but still, four out of nine?"

"It kind of always bothered me that master mages could be killed by a vamp," I said. "Du Mont was tough, but how did she get past their shields?"

The Master sighed. "Gerald Lazenby was Diana's partner,

but it was well-known that he was a womanizer. He also liked—how shall I put this—a little bit of rough."

It took me a moment to understand. "You mean, like the women on East Colfax?"

"Yeah, that's what he means," Dierdre said.

Madeleine had spent some time on East Colfax, but her interests were a little different than the hookers. She took payment in blood. The exsanguinated bodies of some prominent Queen City businessmen were part of the reason she initially drew the attention of the Mayor's office, and subsequently the Guild.

"And the other person? Donita?" I asked.

"Donita Simpson was always a bit careless about her personal security," Master Greenwood said. "She lived in an old mansion near the Capitol, and as best as we could tell, was ambushed on her front doorstep."

"And who was the other Council member who died?"

"Thomas Fairchild. A geomancer and businessman. Chairman of Front Range Mining Corporation. Founded the company back in the twenties. Nineteen twenties. He was killed in an accident at one of his mines up in the mountains. No one questioned it at the time, but now I'm wondering if it really was an accident."

A geomancer killed in a mining accident. Obviously, the Guild was a lot less suspicious than I was.

CHAPTER 39

I tried calling Loretta, but my attempt went to voicemail after three rings. Master Greenwood had his servants fix us a meal of steak slices in a mushroom cream sauce over noodles with roasted vegetables. While we ate, we monitored three TV sets. The city was a mess, and so was the reporting.

It was the first time I met the three women who were rumored to be Master Greenwood's concubines. Doris Scanlon appeared to be in her forties, with short dark hair and brown eyes. Her aura was that of an aeromancer. Elise Adams, a hydromancer, had shoulder-length amber-blonde hair, blue eyes, and a classic hourglass figure. She appeared to be about the same age as Dierdre. Amelia Sorento was a tiny, slender Italian woman with waist-length straight black hair. I guessed her as being at least in her seventies—but I hoped I looked that good at forty —and her aura showed almost as much fire as Jodi's.

They all acted as though they had met me before, but I knew that wasn't the case. Of course, the earthquake was the obvious topic of conversation.

A second call to Loretta likewise went unanswered, and I didn't have Adelheid Bauer's number. When I called Scott, he said both his dojo and his house had very little damage, but that he was canceling the tournament. Delia answered my call to the yarn shop. She and Jodi were all right, but they didn't have water or heat. The authorities turned off the gas lines in most of the city until they could be inspected. The weather was warm enough that fixing the water lines was the first priority.

It was after sunset when I finally got an answer on Loretta's phone, but it was Adelheid who answered.

"We're at QC General," she said. "Loretta has a broken leg and a concussion, but the doctors say she'll be fine. I'm a little shaken up, but okay. I'm sorry I couldn't trace your summoner, but I'm going looking for that mage who caused the earthquake."

"You saw him? You can identify him? I was too far away."

"Oh, yes, I will know him if I see him again," she said, and the tone of her voice left no doubt she planned to make him pay.

"Don't try to take him on alone," I said.

"Well, I have to get Loretta out of here, and that won't be until tomorrow. She told me that her place has stairs."

That was said with a bit of a hopeful cant.

"My place is on the third floor," I replied. "No elevator."

A sigh. "Well, I guess I'll put her up in my spare room. You remember how to get to my place?"

"Yeah. Call me and I'll come by."

※

The following morning, I waited until nine o'clock, then called Loretta's number. To my surprise, she answered.

"How are you feeling?" I asked.

"Like crap. The leg aches, and I feel like I've been beaten up by a pack of werewolves. I'm also hungry, and I don't even know where to look in her kitchen. I'm not sure if some of the stuff in the fridge is food or ingredients for a casting."

"You have electricity? Where's Adelheid?"

"Yeah, we have power. She went out earlier. I expected her back by now."

"Crap! I'll call you later."

I went looking for Dierdre.

"I need to get into town."

"Good luck. A huge number of streets are closed, and the ones that are open are jammed with traffic. Or they're cracked and full of debris."

After I explained the problem, I ended up in a Range Rover with her and Amelia. We stopped by a grocery store on the far west side, and I picked up a couple of bags of groceries that would keep for a few days without refrigeration. Then we made our way to Adelheid's house. Loretta's pickup was parked in front of the house. I ran in with the groceries.

"Oh, bless you!" Loretta said when I dropped the food on the coffee table next to the recliner where she sat.

"She isn't back yet?"

"No. I tried to call her, and it just goes to voicemail."

"What kind of car does she drive?"

"An old, old Volkswagen. Sort of a faded lime green. She took it when she left."

"Any idea where she went?"

Loretta shook her head. "She just said that the quake was caused by a Guild mage, and she was going to find him."

I shot out of there and into the Range Rover.

"Carlisle Square," I said as I buckled my seat belt. "Adelheid has gone hunting the mage that caused the quake."

"Not smart," Amelia said. "I don't care how old and wise she might be, there's a qualitative difference between a mage's power and that of a witch. And the bastard who's causing these quakes has power."

"Loretta told me that Adelheid moved to Queen City in the mid-1800s. The main streets were still mud."

"Then she should know better than to go hunting a master mage," Amelia said.

"And geomancers are tricky," Dierdre said. "Kaitlyn, cast your shield far out from your body anytime you confront a geomancer. You want to protect your oxygen supply."

"Do you think Master O'Hara survived?" I asked.

Dierdre clenched her jaw, then shook her head. "He might be able to survive being swallowed by the earth, but whether he can survive wherever that demon took him, I don't know."

It was only two or three miles from Adelheid's house to Carlisle Square, but it took us more than an hour. Twice we had to back up several blocks and try a different path. The civil authorities had many roads blocked. Then I saw an old VW bug parked at the entrance to an alley.

"Stop! I think that's her car."

I jumped out. Yes, it was Adelheid's, and I could follow her magical signature. She didn't take a direct route toward the Square, and I soon figured out that she probably had some talent as a tracker.

Dierdre and Amelia flanked me, and I realized they were acting as my bodyguards. I followed the scent of the old witch for several blocks, and then less than fifty yards from the Guild Hall, I saw what looked to be black fabric lying on the sidewalk. A dress, fluttering a bit in the soft breeze.

If only Adelheid had waited. She hadn't been dead long. Her body was still warm, and rigor mortis hadn't set in. She was lying face down, and I tried to turn her over. That's when I discovered she was embedded in the concrete. It was like she had lain down and someone poured cement around her. But I knew that wasn't the case. It had turned liquid around her, and she had either fallen or been knocked forward, then the ground hardened.

"Do you understand what I said about your shield?" Dierdre asked me.

"We'll need to get another geomancer to free her," Amelia said. "Until we do that, we won't know how she died."

"I don't suppose you can trace the magic wielder?" Dierdre asked.

I shook my head. "He laid a trap, but he wasn't physically here. I don't feel him at all. The spell was cast from some distance."

It was probably inappropriate, but my thoughts went to Adelheid's cats. Someone would have to take care of them. Did witches really have familiars, or were they only cats?

CHAPTER 40

Amelia went to the Guild Hall to find a geomancer while Dierdre and I stayed with the old witch's body. As I watched Amelia walk away, I allowed my curiosity to ask about Master Greenwood. He was my mentor, possibly my savior, but I knew so little about him.

"Your father keeps an interesting house," I said.

Dierdre snorted. "You might say that. Amelia has lived with him my entire life. My mother died when I was born, but Amelia was already living there. She hasn't really been a mother to me, more like an older sister. Doris showed up when I was in high school, and Elise was my roommate in college." She chuckled. "Greenwood Manor is like a hen house. Other than my father, and Alberto the butler, there are seven women living there. Four servants, including two in the kitchen. Elise moved into my old room, because I never wanted to move back."

"It kind of seems like a harem."

"Yeah, but not really. They all have their own interests, and Dad really isn't a dominant sort of man. They aren't dependent on him, and I know that both Elise and Amelia have had other lovers."

"Where is your house?" I asked.

"I have a cabin on Evergreen Lake. I probably spend two-thirds of my time at the Guild Hall, though."

So, thirty miles up in the mountains, but the area was still serviced by the regional bus line, and her cabin probably was as expensive as a luxury high-rise apartment in the downtown area. If I was curious about her before, I was super curious about what she called a 'cabin.'

"You know, you never have told me what you actually do at the Guild, other than babysit me and Marlene."

She laughed. "My official title is Executive Assistant to the Council. Fancy gofer. Which is actually what I use Marlene for about half her time. Talk about being low on the totem pole. Assistant to the Executive Assistant." She laughed again. "You haven't been with us for any of the major social events. Beltane is coming, though, and I'm in charge of the Guild's Beltane celebration. And then Solstice next after that, then Samhain, Winter Solstice. You'll love it. I'll have you so busy that you won't have time to breathe."

Dierdre turned her gaze to the mountains, and was quiet for a while, then said, "And of course, any special projects that Father or Diana come up with. Things they would do if they had time." She turned a soft smile toward me. "You, for instance. And I must admit, you're the most interesting project they've handed me in a very long time."

"Did you know my parents?"

"Yes, I grew up with your mother."

"Why is my grandmother like that? Why does she hate me so much? Why did she hate my father?"

"Your grandparents are very old-fashioned. They grew up in aristocratic society in late 1900s England. And the magical aristocracy in England is about as snooty as you can get. You know that Carlisle Square was named after your grandfather's family, right? Carlisle Bank and Trust is owned by your family."

"Yeah, lot of good that does me." It was my great-grandfather's older brother who founded the bank in Queen City. The oldest brother, Lord Carlisle, inherited the title and ran the bank in London. My grandfather was a younger son who came to America to work in the bank in QC, ended up running it, and was now retired.

"Well, your mom was engaged to a man from another old Guild family. And then your father showed up. Lee and Sarah, well, I never saw two people more in love. So, Sarah broke off her engagement, and when your grandmother went ballistic, they eloped and got married."

"I heard my grandmother call my father a savage, once."

Dierdre sighed. "He was Irish. His family were deeply involved in the Irish independence movement, and your grandmother's father was killed while he was a member of the English government in Ireland."

"That was so long ago. And what the hell do I have to do with all that?"

"People aren't always rational, Kaitlyn. Just because someone has a lot of magic power doesn't mean their mind works logically."

I shrugged. "Well, thanks. That sort of explains a lot of things. I mean, no one really explains that sort of thing to a kid, do they? Just out of curiosity, who was the guy Mom was engaged to? Anyone I might have met?"

"Oh, yeah. Leon Rathske. I'm not sure he ever got over it. I think he hated your dad."

And he was a powerful geomancer. Who had a fixation on me, a girl who looked like my mother did when he fell in love with her. And when I tried to find out if there was a geomancer with an axe to grind, the Guild had blocked me at every turn.

"What does it mean when someone has a black border to their aura?" I asked.

Dierdre shook her head. "I'm not sure. It's not common,

but I'm not an aura expert." The look on her face told me that she didn't think it was something good.

Amelia returned with half a dozen people, among them Master Rathske.

"Oh, my," he said, staring down at Adelheid. He knelt down and placed his hand flat on either side of her head. I felt magic flow, and opened myself up to the ley line. Rathske pulled brown threads and sent them into the ground around the witch, and it gradually changed.

The magic was very much like that of the mage who caused the earthquake. But I had felt earth magic being used only twice. Could I tell the difference between Dierdre's air magic and that of the mage who attacked me? I didn't know.

"Pull her out," Rathske said. "Don't get too close to her, but grab her arms and pull her straight up as much as you can."

Several people reached for her.

"No, no, not her legs. Pull her head and torso out first, and her legs will follow."

Liquid concrete dripped from Adelheid's body and face. I saw her face as the concrete slipped away, falling back into the body-shaped hole. Her eyes and mouth were wide open, the expression on her face one of shocked terror. She knew she was going to suffocate, and there was nothing she could do about it.

Amelia came and stood next to me, taking hold of my arm.

"Did any of the substance get into her lungs? Did she breathe any of it or swallow it?"

I looked down at her. "How am I supposed to know?"

She pressed her lips together, then said, "I can't teach you a technique I don't understand, child. Use your magic, and look inside her."

So, I tried to see inside a dead woman's body. I gasped.

"What did you see?" Amelia calmly asked.

"No, no solid substance past her mouth. She didn't swallow any of it."

Amelia nodded, a satisfied look on her face.

"What? Why are you looking like the cat who ate the canary?"

She didn't answer, but moved away from me and said something to Dierdre, who bent down to hear Amelia's whisper.

Dierdre turned her head to look at me as she listened. Then she gave Amelia a short reply, and turned back to the group looking at the corpse.

Amelia walked back to me. "Dierdre says you are old for your age. I know a man who lives in Switzerland who has your magic. I shall talk to him. But to my knowledge, he has mentored only two mages in my lifetime. You must want to learn very badly, and work hard at it, or he will send you away. Do you want to learn?"

To my surprise, my eyes misted up, and I felt tears on my cheeks. I didn't know why.

"I just want to understand. I have so many questions, and there are so few answers. What did I just do? How did I do it?"

"I shall talk to him, and in the meantime, your new family—me and Dierdre and Elias and the others—shall prepare you to meet him if he agrees."

"And if he doesn't?"

She shrugged. "Then we'll find someone else. You deserve proper training." She searched my face with her eyes. "But I think my grandfather will say yes."

CHAPTER 41

On the way back to Master Greenwood's mansion, I was bursting with questions. But I wasn't sure what to ask first, or on what topic. Why had Dierdre, Master Greenwood, and Master Olinsky blocked any investigation into Master Rathske? Or were they investigating him themselves, and didn't want me muddling things up?

I didn't even know what the internal Guild laws were. They certainly couldn't turn him over to the mundane civil authorities. The idea of locking a geomancer up in a steel and concrete prison was absurd.

And if Rathske was causing the earthquakes, who was the aeromancer that had attacked me? And, of course, there was the minor issue of who was summoning the demon? And why only that same fire demon every time? It made me think the summoner was basically an amateur who stumbled across a ritual and a name.

"If I wanted to summon a demon, how difficult would it be to find a name?" I asked. "I know that summoning rituals are available on the internet, and probably on the back of breakfast cereal boxes. If it doesn't work, then try the next ritual Google brings up. But it's the name that's the stumbling block, isn't it?"

Amelia chuckled in the back seat.

"I told you she was sharp," Dierdre said. "Yes, the name. And you're right about the rituals. The ritual that the summoner is using works with this particular demon."

"There may be demons that could be summoned using that ritual," Amelia said, "but not controlled. That would put the summoner in a very precarious situation. From everything I've seen, this demon is either young or weak. Since our knowledge of demons is very scarce, we can't determine which."

"Weak?" My voice came out kind of squeaky.

"Why, yes. There have been demons that took over entire kingdoms and brought their minions over from the other plane. We have a problem, but not one it will take an army of mages to solve. We just have to kill one summoner."

"Or one demon," Dierdre said, "but it's probably easier to kill the summoner."

We rode along for a while, then I said, "That's what you'll do with the summoner? Kill her?"

"Do you have another solution?" Amelia asked. "A lobotomy, perhaps? Chain her—you did say her, didn't you—to a rock in a cave on a desert island and leave her until she starves to death? Send her to knitting classes for rehabilitation?"

She leaned over the seat so she could see my face. "Make no mistake, people who cause earthquakes and call demons are not nice people. I could set this city on fire, but I don't. If I did, the only logical solution would be to shoot me like a mad dog. Do you have any idea how close we all are to having the Guild Hall nuked? All of us hunted down? Burned at the stake?"

She sat back, and I could see her in the rearview mirror—arms crossed, staring out the window, and I didn't even have words for the expression on her face. Anger, yes, but also fear and disbelief. I looked out at the devastation we drove through.

Rubble and toppled trees. Broken and cracked pavement. A car under a collapsed wall. A child's doll lying alone in a driveway of a house with all its windows broken.

"Adelheid, the witch that died, said the summoner was female," I said. "She was at the summoning site. I don't know what else she was able to scry, but she probably talked to Loretta. The question is, how much does Loretta remember after a concussion."

Master Greenwood's estate showed no evidence of being anywhere near an earthquake. Dierdre parked the Range Rover on the side of the house.

"Look," I said, twisting in my seat so I could look at both Dierdre and Amelia, "suppose all of this is just crazy shit, with no real purpose at all. Rathske is causing earthquakes because he couldn't have my mom and I won't even get close enough to touch when he's handing out money. And the summoner is taking out her revenge on the Guild for rejecting her, or someone on the Council not acknowledging paternity, or not paying for her tuition. I mean, look at history. People have started wars for less."

Amelia stared at me for at least a minute or two, then said, "Libraries are dry and warm on stormy days, aren't they?" Her voice was so devoid of any emotion, I felt the trees around us shudder.

She turned to Dierdre. "You know, it is kind of foolish to rule out anything at this point. Hell, if you told me magic and demons were involved, I'd be inclined to believe you."

She opened her door, got out of the car, and walked slowly to the nearest door of the house.

CHAPTER 42

After poring over the city's disaster map, I armed myself and took off to find the street kids I knew. When I reached the part of town where they had hung out through the winter, I found a place to sit on what was left of a warehouse wall.

Queen City had never built with a concern about major earthquakes, and the homeless took advantage of abandoned warehouses and other buildings for shelter in the winter. I knew from news reports that the area was hit hard, but I wasn't prepared for the devastation in front of me. Even buildings that still stood looked as though a stiff wind would finish their collapse.

Basically, it looked like pictures I had seen of cities that had been bombed in a war. On TV, they showed people and machinery digging through rubble, searching for survivors. There weren't any searchers or equipment where I was. Occasionally, a bird called.

For most people, the phrase 'street kids' conjured the image of drugged out pickpockets. Gangbangers, druggies, and criminals. But the abuse some kids endured was so horrific it made the streets preferable. I had seen some of the damage, and occasionally, some of them talked about their experiences.

I hit the streets at fourteen—almost six feet tall—with four years of karate lessons, some weapons training, a major attitude, and more bravado than sense. It took me a while to figure out the whole survival thing, and figure out my magic, before I ended up on the top of the youth hierarchy. But like the other kids, I stayed away from adults when I could.

I stepped over a pile of bricks and found a Raggedy Ann doll. I couldn't breathe, and just stared at it. Then I sat down and cried. After about fifteen minutes, I dug through the bricks, dreading what I might find. The little girl who lost her doll wasn't there. I put the doll in my bag and continued my search.

More than two hours after I started my search, I found a camp. The walls of an old warehouse had collapsed and crushed four kids, ages approximately fifteen to maybe seventeen. Their bedding, some spare clothing, a little bit of pot, and some canned food comprised their possessions.

Dierdre picked up on the second ring. "Where are you?"

"The old warehouse district north of downtown. Near the train tracks. I've found some bodies. There may be kids who survived. Do you suppose anyone might send a dog or a mage or someone over here?" My voice caught on the last sentence, and I felt the tears on my cheeks again. "Maybe someone cares if anyone here may need some help?"

"I'll see what I can do. Are you all right?"

"Oh, yeah. I'm not dumb enough to go into most of these places. It's like a war zone."

I hung up, then tore a scrap of a red skirt from one of the girls, and used a piece of rebar to make a flag to mark the spot.

Half an hour later, I reached the warehouse where the kids I knew had sheltered from the blizzard. Half of it was still standing, but the upper floors had mostly collapsed. I sniffed around, calling out, and detected some signs that people might have been there during the quake. Then, from a hole in a pile of bricks, a voice.

"Hey! Do you have any water?" The voice of a young girl.

"Yeah, I do. Where are you?"

A head poked out of the hole. "Oh, wow! It's Katy Brown!" She scrambled out and ran toward me. I caught her up in a hug, and she squeezed me so hard I thought she might break something. It was Caro, the girl with the vamp-chewed arm. Another face appeared in the hole—Lisa.

"Are you kids all right?" I asked.

"I'm okay, and so's Lisa," she said, "Just awful thirsty. But Ginny's caught—her leg—and we can't get her out."

I walked back to the hole with her. It didn't look as though I could fit, especially with my weapons.

"Just the three of you?"

She nodded. "Jeremy's dead."

I tapped the ley line, pulled white threads, and began floating bricks away from the pile. It took me forever to enlarge the hole and crawl in. I shined a flashlight in and found that they had been camping under a steel beam in a small room—probably an office. When the quake brought the roof down, the beam caught on the outside wall, then flooring from the upper floor fell onto the beam, and bricks fell onto that flooring. It created a cave, and the only reason any of them survived.

Ginny's leg was crushed by the steel beam. She was unconscious, which was a blessing, but her breathing was shallow, her face was flushed and hot. It didn't appear she had lost much blood, but I wasn't placing any bets on whether she would keep the leg. On the other side of the opening was a boy about my age who was obviously dead, a chunk of brick embedded in his skull.

"Has she been awake at all?" I asked.

"Yeah," Lisa said, "but she's been out for a couple of hours, and she was in a lot of pain when she was awake. We tried to move the bricks around her, but this cave isn't very stable. We were afraid we'd bring the whole thing down."

I backed out and called Dierdre. When she answered, I explained the problem.

"Can you cast a shield on the inside of the cave?" she asked when I finished.

"Yeah, but that steel beam is lying right on her leg. There isn't any separation. If I bring the ceiling down, I don't know if my shield would hold."

"Leave your phone on. I'll be there as soon as I can," she said.

We sat on a pile of rubble outside their cave. I passed around my water bottle, and we sat and waited. While we did that, I cast a projection of Master Rathske.

"Is that the guy who took Simone?" I asked.

Both girls shook their heads.

"It looks a lot like him," Lisa said, "but the guy who comes here sometimes is younger and thinner. They could almost be brothers, though."

Caro nodded. So much for that theory. Could Rathske have an accomplice? The aeromancer? Most likely the summoner.

A helicopter flew over us, and when I looked up, I saw that it had the Guild's emblem on the side. A blonde woman looked out of an open door, and then jumped. My heart seemed to skip a beat, but Dierdre floated down and landed as though she had simply taken the last step off some stairs. A large bag was thrown from the copter, and it also floated down to the ground.

"Where's your problem?" Dierdre asked.

I pointed to the hole, and she dove into it without any hesitation. I noticed that she was wearing her normal silk shirt and designer jeans. She hadn't even taken time to change, and my respect for her increased even more.

"Kaitlyn, drag that bag over here and hand me stuff as I ask for it."

I dragged the bag over and unzipped it. It contained a couple of blankets, gauze, bandages, surgical tape, multiple bottles of pills, and a box with syringes and vials.

"There's a box with syringes," she said. I pushed it into the hole and she grabbed it. I saw that she had cast some kind of magical light inside the small cave. I pulled the bag after me into the cave.

Dierdre gave Ginny an injection in her upper arm, then three injections in her thigh from a different syringe.

"Cast your shield," Dierdre ordered. "I want it to outline this entire space. And hold it."

I did as she directed, then she said, "Tell those girls to get as far away from us as they can."

"Caro! You and Lisa back off! Back way off!"

I saw Dierdre pull white threads from the ley line.

"Okay, Kaitlyn, I'm going to expand this room like a balloon, and I need you to expand your shield as I do so. You can see what I'm doing, right?"

"Yeah."

"Okay, now, slowly."

I could see the white magical threads fill the space we were in and then begin to push at the bricks and dirt and steel around us. And just like a balloon, the space expanded. The beam lifted off Ginny's leg, and Dierdre pulled her free.

"Katy, get her out of here. Now! I'll hold the roof."

I grabbed the girl under her arms and backed out. Her leg was a mangled mess, and it left a smear of blood and flesh on the ground behind her. Once I got us out, I called, "Dierdre, we're free!"

My mentor backed out of the hole, pulling the bag of equipment behind her. Once we were about ten feet away, I saw her let go of the strands of magic, and the little cave collapsed.

"Send down the basket!" Dierdre's voice was louder than the helicopter. She glanced over at me and winked. "Air magic."

Someone pushed the rescue basket out of the helicopter door and lowered it. Dierdre and I carried the girl to it and tucked the blanket in the basket around her. We stepped back, and the crew inside began to winch the basket up.

Dierdre was on her phone. "Get her to an emergency room stat! No, I'll stay. I'll call you if I need you again."

The 'copter rose into the sky and turned in the direction of the Guild Hall.

"Well, shall we see what else we can find?" Dierdre asked.

We all had a lunch of some energy bars, then went looking for more survivors. A couple of hours later, Dierdre called the helicopter back, and it landed in an open area. Master Olinsky was there and watched as we loaded four more injured kids on it. Dierdre and I stayed until someone brought her dad's Range Rover out with supplies for the twenty kids in the little encampment we had helped to organize.

CHAPTER 43

"They're children!" Dierdre said.

We were eating dinner at the Greenwood mansion with the Master and his three ladies.

"What did you think I was talking about?" I asked. "Street kids. Kids who live on the street."

"It's one thing to know it intellectually, but they should be playing with dolls!"

"Did you find out anything?" Master Greenwood asked.

"Well, I showed Lisa and Caro a projection. They were with Simone when that man lured her away. But they said that wasn't the man."

"What did you show them?" Amelia asked.

I placed a projection of Master Rathske in the middle of the table. It caused a lot of raised eyebrows.

"And what did they say?" Master Greenwood asked.

"Not him. The guy was younger, thinner. But they did say they resembled each other."

"I'm missing something," Doris said.

"One of the sacrifices was a young girl that Kaitlyn knew,"

Dierdre explained. "She was lured into going off with a man on promise of some money."

"A hundred bucks," I said. "That would have fed the three of them for a couple of weeks."

"And she was how old?" Doris asked.

"Fifteen." I took a deep breath. "Kids living on the street don't believe in altruism. Any adult that offers to help them is automatically assumed to be a pedophile or a social worker—which sometimes is worse. But when your belly is so empty that it hurts, or it's so cold you can't feel your feet, you take chances you know aren't smart, and you do things you don't want to. As a guy said to me the night I first met Caro and Lisa, letting a pervert bugger him was better than going home where his father beat him."

Doris paled, and Elise and Marlene suddenly looked sick.

"Probably not the best dinner table conversation," I said, feeling my face warm, and returned my attention to my meal.

The Master looked across the table at his daughter, and Dierdre gave a barely perceptible nod.

※

The Master's house had eight bedrooms, plus four more in the servants' quarters. I was shown to a room after dinner and discovered it had its own bathroom, and a closet full of clothes that fit me. That didn't surprise me overmuch, since Dierdre was two or three inches taller than I was. But Dierdre probably couldn't button those tops. Maybe they were hers when she was my age.

I was getting ready to pour myself a bath when there was a knock at the door. One of the maids said I was to attend the Master in his study. I was already undressed, but I slipped on a pair of clean jeans and a bathrobe, and followed her downstairs.

She showed me into the study, where I found the Master, Dierdre, and Amelia.

My face flamed. "I'm sorry. I was in the process of pouring a bath. It's been a rather filthy day."

"I can sympathize," Dierdre said, and I realized she was also wrapped in a bathrobe.

"I want to talk about that image you showed the girls, and the answers they gave you," the Master said. "Kaitlyn, I understand that you don't care for Master Rathske, but you need to be discreet about any accusations."

I bit my lip, and considered my answer. When I had my temper under control, I said, "You met my friend Jodi."

Dierdre and the Master nodded.

"What Jodi said after meeting Master Rathske was, and I quote, 'If that bastard ever touches me, I'll light him up.' Now, you may consider her a little girl, but I think you should consider whether a pyromancer can turn a geomancer into a piece of pottery. She tried to fight our demon, and it didn't want any part of her."

Amelia snorted, then choked on her laughter.

"We know we have a geomancer problem," I continued, "but every time I try to bring it up, I get brushed off. If not Rathske, then who? And does Rathske have a brother? Nephew? Nothing makes sense. They don't have these problems in Dallas or Phoenix or Vegas or anywhere else. I watch the news. You hired me to track a summoner. If you want me to stop, then I'm going to hitchhike to Laramie and hang out there for the summer."

"While you were gone today," Amelia said very quietly, "we had another demon manifestation. The demon targeted QC General Hospital. It flattened the wing where your friend Loretta Lighthorse was treated, along with about a hundred and fifty other people."

I shook my head. "Adelheid helped Loretta check out—

although not officially. They took a service elevator. So she wasn't there. Who else—I mean trackers, witches, or mages—was in that hospital?" I asked. "I think we can rule out that this demon is just conjured randomly because someone gets bored."

The Master wrote on the pad in front of him. "I'll check."

"You might also check and see who was out of town on days of the demon appearances, the earthquakes, tornadoes—you know, that sort of thing," Dierdre said. "At the very least, we can eliminate some suspects."

"I didn't know you kept that close an eye on people," I said.

"We don't. And if I tell you and Marlene and Dad I'm going to Vail, and I don't go, or go somewhere else, the Guild wouldn't know where I was. But we've been dealing with this crap for two months now, and we really aren't any closer to fixing it. Thousands of people dying isn't a good look for the Guild."

And people like Ginny and Loretta and Adelheid were suffering for it. Back in my room, I turned on the TV while the bathtub filled. One wing of the hospital—six stories—was flattened. The newscaster said it had not been damaged by the quake, or at least not very much. The demon had danced on it until nothing was left.

One of the people the camera caught walking around had white-blonde hair. The camera wasn't on her very long, but I could tell the hairstyle and clothing were the same as the dhampir. Loretta seemed to have some kind of issue with the woman. I wondered if the woman had an issue with Loretta.

CHAPTER 44

The following morning, I knocked at the open door of Master Greenwood's study. "Master? I have some questions about dhampir."

"Come in. I'm really not an expert on them, but I'll try to help you out."

I sat down in a chair in front of his desk.

"There is a woman, and at first I thought she might be following me, but Loretta and I finally decided we were just coincidentally sometimes in the same places." I went on to tell him about the mystery woman, and Loretta's belief she was a dhampir.

"And you think your friend Loretta is a dhampir," he said when I finished.

"Their auras are almost identical. The differences could be explained by the difference in their mothers' magic. Loretta's mother was a witch, and I'm thinking the blonde woman's mother was a mage."

"Can you show me a projection of her?"

I projected her as I'd seen her in the diner. The reaction was not what I expected.

"Oh, bloody hell!" he exclaimed. He peered at the image, then fell back into his chair, and continued to stare at it. "This woman is here, in Queen City?"

"Yes. Do you know her?"

"Not exactly. Please, don't show this to anyone else." He shrugged, then said, "Not that most people would recognize her. Kaitlyn, you know that humans can become addicted to the chemicals released when a vampire feeds on them, right?"

I nodded. "Sure. That's how they get their blood whores."

"Well, it is also addictive for vampires to feed on mages. Mage blood gets them higher than a kite. But over time, it also drives them mad. It upsets the chemical balance in their brains, or at least that's the accepted theory. With me so far?"

"Yeah, I think so."

"Okay. I'm going to tell you a story. Once upon a time—" there was a twinkle in his eye, and I saw the corner of his mouth lift a little bit.

I burst out laughing, and he chuckled.

"Is this part of your experience with little girls?" I asked.

"Some things that seem clichéd have a sound logical reason behind them. I got your attention, didn't I?"

I nodded, smiling.

"Okay. Once upon a time, there was a powerful mage. She had lived a long time, had a husband and children, but now she was growing older, and she was alone. She took a lover, a much younger man. Now, I'm not sure exactly what happened next, but he was turned by a vampire. I don't know if he was attacked, or perhaps he had a vampire lover, but he was turned. The mage did not know this at first, but she was in love, and kept him in her bed. She ended up being his blood whore, and she got pregnant."

He cocked his head and raised an eyebrow. "Are you with me?"

"Yes, she gave birth and died, right?"

"That's right. By that time, her lover was thoroughly addicted to mage blood, and more than a little crazy. When she died, he took the baby and disappeared. Until today, nobody here in the Guild had any idea where that little girl had gone."

"You think the woman I showed you is that girl."

"The woman you showed me died in childbirth thirty-two years ago. Since I'm sure she died, I can only assume the woman you showed me is her daughter."

"Okay, but what's the scandal? I assume that since thirty-two years have passed, no one should be completely freaked out by her showing up now.

"This is the part you have to understand, and keep completely to yourself. That woman may be Diana Olinsky's half-sister. I'm going to want you to accompany me to talk to Master Olinsky and show her your projection."

Holy shit. And what if I was correct, and she was the summoner? I remembered Master Olinsky telling me to project illusions when she tested me. She knew how accurate they were. Jodi had what they called an eidetic memory. I had something like that but for images, things I'd seen.

"Yes, sir. Uh, when?"

"Probably not right now. I'm sure she's more than a little busy, but I'm supposed to meet her at the Mayor's office this afternoon. I'll see where we can fit you into her schedule."

"So, I'm free to go snooping today?"

He chuckled. "Yes, but be careful. Do you have anyone to watch your back?"

"I was thinking of taking Jodi with me."

"You need to get that girl into the Guild as soon as possible. She's as much of a potential disaster as any demon."

That took me by surprise, and hurt me. "She's really sweet."

"And completely untrained. The thought of the two of you trying to take on that demon keeps me awake sometimes. I can't believe you did that." He leaned over his desk. "Kaitlyn, your magic is important, and the fact that you care about people makes it even more so. The same with that little flame-haired shadow of yours. The Guild needs people like you. The world needs people like you. Don't get yourself killed."

"I'll do my best, sir."

※

I checked with the kitchen staff to see if anyone was going into town and hitched a ride with one of the cooks going to the grocery store. From there, I caught a bus, and although many of the bus routes were disrupted, I managed to ride to within a mile of the yarn shop.

The neighborhood was three or four miles from the Capitol. At first, everything seemed normal, but if I looked closer, I could see some buckled sidewalks and cracks in a few houses. But all the windows were intact.

The yarn shop was closed. I pushed the doorbell and knocked. I could hear movement inside, and then Delia opened the door. She didn't seem particularly happy to see me.

"Jodi! Your friend is here!" she shouted, then turned and walked away.

Jodi came from a back room, and skipped the rest of the way when she saw me.

"So glad to see you!"

I leaned down and said very quietly, "I'm going looking for someone I think is the summoner. Want to come? I'll buy dinner."

She nodded vigorously. "Sure thing. Let me change my shoes."

She took off upstairs, and Delia stood by the counter, staring at me.

"You're going to give her to the Guild, aren't you?" she asked.

"I'm not giving her to anyone. I think that's where she should be, and I'll tell her that. She needs training, and she's much too powerful to just let her learn on her own."

Delia harrumphed at me.

"For God's sake, Delia. She's fourteen! You're not even pretending to be her mom. You don't even send her to school. You're walking a fine line. All it would take is one phone call from a busybody and you'd be in jail and she'd be in the system. They would contact her real mom. She's managed to avoid that for two years. Give her a chance to grow up and decide for herself who and what she wants to be."

"I guess you'd know about busybodies."

I took a deep breath. "I know about pedophiles. I was her age when I hit the street."

She jerked as though I'd slapped her. Jodi came down the stairs at that moment, carrying a wind breaker and wearing hiking boots rather than the tennis shoes she was wearing earlier.

"Katy is treating me to dinner," Jodi said, "so I'll be home after that."

I looked back at Delia as I closed the door behind us. She stood there, stone faced with her arms crossed.

CHAPTER 45

"So, you found the summoner?"
"I've identified someone I think might be the summoner. I don't know who she is, or where she lives, but I want to find out. Jodi, this could be dangerous. You know my friend Loretta? The lady who was working with me? The demon squashed the hospital where she was treated after the earthquake."

Her expression changed from excited to very solemn.

"Now, here's what I want to do." I continued. "I'm going to try and sniff her out, and I want you to follow me. I don't want anyone to know that we're together, okay? I'm hoping you'll be able to spot her if she's tailing me."

I projected the image of the blonde woman. Then I handed Jodi a burner phone I'd picked up on the way to her house. I had programmed in my number on the speed dial.

"If you see her, call me."
"Got it."
"How much can you control your flame?" I asked. "I mean, can you project a tight beam that doesn't set the whole neighborhood on fire?"

She laughed, then extended her arm and index finger. A white-hot flame erupted from her finger and burned a hole in the brick wall across the street.

"Will that do?" she asked with a cocky grin. "I can do fireballs, too, but I can't throw them very far."

Both Jodi and I stood out in a crowd, but for different reasons. I for my height, and she for her hair and incredible looks. But she was so young that no one would consider her a threat, or that she was doing any kind of adult thing.

We took a bus, not sitting together, down to QC General. I wandered around, visiting the areas where I had seen the blonde woman on TV. I couldn't pick up any magical scent, but I could trace the demon's path back the way it came.

We ended up at Lincoln Park, and I called Jodi.

"I think this is too much of a coincidence," I told her. "I'll bet she lives around here."

I also wondered about her motivations. Master Olinsky was meeting with the Mayor that afternoon. At least a couple of demon manifestations could be considered to be aimed at her.

Something I had noticed about Loretta was that her magical signature was so faint that I couldn't rely on it to track her, and her scent was almost nonexistent. The other dhampir was probably the same. But there was the summoner's magical scent, which was the same in Lincoln Park that day as it had been at all the other summonings. I needed something of hers.

But instead of following the woman to the bus stop, which I knew would be a dead end, I wandered out in a spiral pattern into the neighborhood around the park. I was thinking there might be another attempt on Master Olinsky, though using the site at Lincoln Park so soon after the hospital catastrophe seemed a bit brash.

I called Jodi again. "Jodi, are there any other places near here where she might have privacy for her ritual?" I asked.

"Maybe one of those parks along Speer Boulevard, but that

would have made more sense for the attack on the hospital. Are there any areas in the quake zone that have been closed off and the emergency personnel have finished searching?"

That was a great idea, and I called Dierdre to ask.

"I know what you're thinking," Dierdre said, "but it wouldn't have to be a park. So many of the downtown and Capitol Hill areas are closed off. Businesses are closed down; apartment buildings and hotels have been evacuated. You saw what things were like when we were looking for your witch friend."

"Could the ritual be done inside a building?" I asked.

"No reason it couldn't. That demon isn't that big. A school gymnasium would work."

"How about the convention center?"

"Completely closed down. Parts of the building were damaged pretty badly. Katy, what are you thinking? That she's going to call the demon again?"

"Master Olinsky and your father are supposed to meet with the Mayor this afternoon. I think someone inside the Guild is feeding the summoner information on the Council's schedules. That disaster at the Capitol was planned to take them out."

I hung up and called Jodi to tell her I was going to make my way north toward the convention center. Even if the summoner couldn't get inside, there was a sculpture garden on the north side, and much closer to City Hall than Lincoln Park, that wasn't very visible from outside. When I was homeless, it was a nice place to hang out on sunny days. That was where I kissed a boy for the first time.

On my way there, I turned down one street and was shocked to find a hot dog cart. I bought one, paid for a second, and said it was for a little redheaded girl who would be along shortly. Then I called Jodi again and told her to pick up her dog when she got there. The normality of the situation put a smile on my face, and I marched on through the rubble eating my hot dog with sauerkraut.

It was eerie, though. I crossed Cherry Creek at Colfax and Speer, and there was no traffic. No one on the streets. Dead quiet except for the birds. The lead story on the national TV news that morning had been Queen City. The earthquake was news, of course, 6.2 on the Richter Scale. But they had also reported on the demon, with video. Queen City looked like hell, or Beirut, on TV.

The mundane community was up in arms. Businesses were threatening the Mayor with pulling out and relocating elsewhere. It seemed the whole world had their eyes on my hometown, and not for good reasons. I wasn't sure exactly why I was still there. It didn't seem to make a lot of sense to stay in a place so dangerous.

I reached the Convention Center and wandered around the side of it, still woolgathering. My phone rang.

"She's right behind you!"

I shielded and turned enough to see the blonde woman before something large, hard, and heavy fell on me, knocking me to the ground. I rolled away from her, drawing my sword as I came to my feet.

She was as tall as I was, maybe a little taller, and the chunk of concrete that clattered to the ground was too heavy for even a vampire to lift. In the back of my mind, I realized she had some aeromancer ability.

I swung low, hoping to take her by surprise, but my sword slid off her shield. I knew that dhampir were faster and stronger than humans, but not as powerful as a vampire. I circled her, hoping to gain an advantage.

A red bolt of flame hit her shield. She whirled around, spotted Jodi, and took off running away from us. By the time I rounded the building, she was out of sight.

My phone rang again. It was Jodi, who said, "Come back around to the sculpture garden."

I sheathed my sword and trotted back in that direction. In a place where two buildings angled together, Jodi sat on a low wall. In front of her, drawn on the pavement, were the ritual circles the summoner had used in the past to call the demon. No sign of her sacrifice, nor had I seen anyone else.

"Pretty good guessing," Jodi said. "I think you've figured out who the summoner is."

"Where's the sacrifice?"

"Maybe it was supposed to be you."

I started to tell her that wasn't funny, but she wasn't smiling.

CHAPTER 46

I called Master Greenwood's cell phone.
"Master? We caught up to that woman I showed you. She was in the act of summoning the demon. She got away, though. Jodi and I are at the sculpture garden behind the Convention Center."

"I can't talk right now. Call Dierdre." He hung up.

So, I did. It rang, she answered by saying, "We're almost there. Give me a couple of minutes." Then she hung up.

I stared at the phone, then looked at Jodi. She shrugged.

The Range Rover pulled up on the street next to the sculpture garden, then drove over the curb and onto the grass, which I knew was absolutely forbidden. Dierdre and Amelia got out and walked toward us.

When they reached us, Jodi pointed to the chalked circles.

"Where's the sacrifice?" Dierdre asked.

Jodi pointed at me.

"It could have been, I guess," I said. "Jodi warned me and I shielded. How did you get here so fast?"

"We've been following you all day," Amelia said. "Not that

easy with all the closed streets. I guess you didn't need us, though."

I projected an image of the blonde woman, including the fangs she had shown me. "She tried to club me with a chunk of concrete the size of Jodi, so I guess she's not only a dhampir but also an aeromancer."

"She looks sort of familiar, but I can't place her," Dierdre said. Amelia just looked thoughtful. Dierdre would have still been a child thirty-two years before.

"The question now is, how do we track her down?" I asked. "I can track humans, vampires, and werewolves, but I've had major problems tracking dhampirs, and her in particular."

"Well, I guess we can inform the police, put out an all-points bulletin for her. Set a Guild bounty," Dierdre said.

"I think you also need to find who is giving her inside information, such as where Masters Olinsky and Greenwood are meeting with the Mayor this afternoon," I said. "She didn't pick this spot at random."

Dierdre gave me a hard narrow-eyed look, but Amelia simply nodded and said, "You think the geomancer and this woman are working together?"

"At least to a certain extent. The demon and a major earthquake just happened at the same time, right? How much are you willing to assign to coincidence?"

Dierdre took a number of pictures of the circle, and samples of the chalk, which she put in plastic bags, then she called a hard wind that scoured the chalk away.

"Have you girls eaten anything?" Amelia asked.

"We had a hot dog," Jodi said. "And Katy's taking me out to dinner."

Dierdre smiled. "I think I can take you both out to dinner. Name the place—" she chuckled, "—any place that's in one piece."

"Spaghetti?" Jodi suggested.

"I know just the place," Amelia said.

She did. It was way out of my price range, and she spoke Italian to the owner who personally waited on us. It was in the damage zone north of downtown in Larimer Square, but the owner grinned and said the damage wasn't as bad as what happened to his restaurant in Naples during World War II. Since he looked to be about fifty, and he was talking about owning a restaurant seventy-five years before, I assumed he was a mage or a witch.

The food was good and plentiful. Just what two teenagers needed after crawling through a war zone all day.

"You're Italian?" I asked Amelia, though I thought it was pretty obvious.

"Swiss, actually. Italian is one of the official languages in Switzerland. Italian was my mother's native language, and German was my father's language. The Guild has one of its largest locations in Geneva, and French is the language they speak there."

"I've seen pictures of the Alps. A lot like Colorado," I said.

"Yes, Switzerland is a lot like Colorado. I met Dierdre's parents there, and they invited me to visit them. I fell in love and I'm still here."

After dinner, we drove Jodi back to the yarn shop. When we got there, Jodi said, "That's strange."

"What?"

"The lights are on in the shop. We live upstairs, and we always turn off the downstairs lights."

She jumped out of the car and ran to the door. Dierdre set the brake, and I got out and followed Jodi. She went to a side door and entered the building. Things were quiet for a little, then I heard her scream.

I drew my short sword and pushed through the door. I could hear Jodi wailing and sobbing in the front room and cautiously went in there.

It was a horror show. Delia was gutted and hanging by one leg upside down from the ceiling. The shelves were pulled down from one wall, and painted in blood there were two words, "Back Off," in letters a foot high. I did notice that the amount of blood in the room was far less than I would expect.

Jodi was on her knees, sobbing, with her face in her hands. I lifted her up, hugged her to me, and pulled her out of the room. We almost ran into Dierdre and Amelia, but I dragged Jodi past them and took her outside.

I kept hold of her arm, pulling her along with me, as I scouted the rest of the property. A neat backyard with a small vegetable garden, and a patio with a small table and a couple of chairs. The gate out to the alley was open, and I cautiously peered out to find no one there.

When we came back to the house, Amelia was waiting for us.

"Dierdre is calling for security," she said. "Jodi, why don't you come with me. We'll sit in the car together until we're sure everything is safe. Check the upstairs," she said to me.

I nodded and went back in the house. I had to go into the front room to reach the stairs, and I tried not to look at the woman hanging there. Upstairs were a fairly large bathroom, a bedroom that appeared to be used only as an office, and the main bedroom. Jodi's clothes were in the office closet. I didn't expect her to come back there, so I looked around and found a couple of suitcases. I gathered all of her clothes that I could find, including shoes, boots, and winter coats, and hauled them downstairs and out to the Range Rover, where I put them in the back.

"There's no reason you need to let the cops know you lived here," I told Jodi. "There's really nothing you can do. Did Delia have any family or anything?"

"Just me," she said.

"Is there anything, papers or whatever, that we should take with us?"

"A small safe. In the office upstairs. It's in the closet behind a panel."

I went back inside and found it behind a hidden panel in the wall. Way too heavy to lift, though. I went downstairs and got Dierdre.

"Jodi says we should take a small safe, but it weighs at least two hundred pounds."

Dierdre nodded and followed me. She lifted the safe out of the wall, carried it downstairs and out to her car—all without ever touching it.

Thirty minutes later, a couple of Guild security cars and a city police car showed up. I let Dierdre deal with them, while Amelia and I kept Jodi in the car.

CHAPTER 47

We drove out to Master Greenwood's estate, and they put Jodi in with me for the night. I held her while she cried herself to sleep, then slipped out of the room. One of the servants brewed me a cup of chamomile tea, and I sat on the terrace looking out over the city. In the middle of the ocean of lights was a large chunk of dark.

The evil of the people who caused that devastation was beyond my understanding.

In the morning, Jodi opened the safe and handed Master Greenwood a large envelope.

"Delia said I was to take this to her lawyer if anything ever happened to her," she said. She also handed the Master a piece of paper. "This is the lawyer's name and address."

Over the next few days, Amelia arranged for Jodi to see a grief counselor at the Guild Hall. She was also scheduled to be tested and admitted into the Guild's school.

"She needs some structure," Amelia told me, "something to replace the life she's known."

I felt a little bit of resentment at that. I wasn't that much older than Jodi was, but everyone treated me like an adult. I had to admit that I would resent it even more had they treated me like a kid, but at the moment I felt like a kid. Or maybe I just wanted to be a kid.

Dierdre worked with me, using her father's overrides, to access data in the computer we hadn't had access to before. Then around noon, she drove me out as close as we could get to the area where I'd found Lisa and Caro before. I managed to find them again, and hand them a backpack full of food that didn't need cooking or refrigeration, along with a bag full of burgers and fries and a couple of jugs of water.

Master Olinsky showed up at the mansion for dinner later that evening, and we ate out on the terrace. After we finished eating, Master Greenwood had me show her the image of the dhampir. She paled, but her expression didn't change in any way I could detect.

"And you think this is the person who murdered that shopkeeper yesterday?" she finally said.

"It's really the only thing that makes sense," I replied. "She had the circles drawn to summon the demon out by the sculpture garden, and we think that if I wasn't shielded, I would have been the next sacrifice. We believe she's been watching me, and when we interrupted her plans, she took her revenge on Jodi."

She was quiet for some time, then said, "Well, that's fairly disturbing. And your explanation for the earthquakes?"

I bit my lip, my eyes darting to Master Greenwood, who gave me a single nod.

"I believe she has an accomplice inside the Guild. I think this is something personal, and a couple of very disturbed people are seeking revenge."

"Very disturbed. Do you mean monstrously psychopathic?"

"Yes, ma'am. That's what I mean."

Amelia leaned across the table. "Imagine what Hitler might have done if he was a powerful mage."

She shot Amelia a look, then said, "Okay, suppose I buy this.

The accomplice inside the Guild, what is his or her motivation?"

"I think he's been seething with the injustice he feels is being done to him, and when someone approached him with a plan to get revenge on the Guild for not making him king, he bought into it. No one has ever appreciated him, he lost the love of his life to a pretender, and even when there are openings on the Council, he's not being considered."

Master Olinsky laughed. "That's what you think, huh? And who is this person who thinks they should be king?"

"Master Rathske. He feels he should have been appointed to the Council, but instead—despite his power and intelligence—he's been denied his proper position by the same woman who has denied the dhampir who tried to kill me today with her proper position and wealth."

She sobered, stared at me, then said, "Oh, that is ridiculous. This is just juvenile pop psychology!"

No one else said anything.

"Yes, it's ridiculous," Master Greenwood finally said, "but no one else has come up with an explanation that makes more sense. It seemed pretty far-fetched to me that Leon would be capable of such things, but you know as well as I do that she's read his character accurately. And we still have no other suspects."

"Most of the older mages aren't in our DNA database," Dierdre said. "But we do have a semen sample from one of the sacrifices. Today, the friends of the girl who was butchered identified the man who lured her away prior to the summoning."

"And his DNA was in our database?" Olinsky asked.

"Yes. And we did get a familial match with the semen."

"And who was this mystery man?"

"Jacob Rathske."

"We also think he's the aeromancer who paid a gang of

young vampires to kill me," I said. "Sort of the same MO as the gang who killed my parents. And we think he was one of the security personnel who got beaten up at that homeless camp the day before the demon destroyed it. He didn't report that he was there, though. One has to wonder why."

Master Olinsky sat quietly for a long time, occasionally glancing around the table at the faces awaiting her reaction.

"I think you're going to get another demon manifestation very soon," Amelia said.

"And we need to ensure it isn't accompanied by an earthquake," Master Greenwood said. "We may even be able to stop the summoning if we can get her location from Leon or his brother. Diana, we have to take the chance. If we're wrong, we haven't lost anything, except perhaps a little face. But if we're right, and we don't act, that would be criminal."

"Do you know who this woman is?" Olinsky obviously aimed the question at me.

"No, and I don't know where she is. She's a dhampir, and I think she's half mage. She can cast a personal shield."

Olinsky looked from me to Dierdre and back. "Don't believe anyone who tells you we don't pay for the sins of our parents."

CHAPTER 48

"Hello, Jacob."
He turned to see who was behind him.
"Surprised? You shouldn't be. I am a tracker, ya know."
I stalked toward him, my sword point weaving a tight figure eight in front of me. "I thought we might have a little chat. Just you and me, without all those pesky vampire friends of yours."
He backed away, and started hammering me with blasts of air. My shield deflected them all.
"For one thing, I wanted to talk to you about your girlfriend. I know she's your girlfriend and not your brother's, because she's way too old for him. But you do procure girls for him, don't you? What a thoughtful little brother. Then your girlfriend uses them for her purposes. But, anyway, where should I find what's-her-name after I kill you? I mean, it seems a shame that you take the blame and pay for all the stuff she and Leon have done."
He turned to run, and discovered an invisible wall. Dierdre and two other aeromancers had him surrounded. He spun back around, and I saw fear cross his face. That added to my rage.
"Now you know what those girls must have felt. Like

Simone. Tell me, did you watch? Is that your gig? You like to watch? Watch your brother have his way with little girls? Watch your girlfriend slit their bellies open while they were still alive? Did they scream? Is that what you get off on? Their terror? You must have known that sooner or later the Guild would catch up to you. You must have known that Leon and your girlfriend would eventually sacrifice you, just like they sacrificed all those other poor fools."

He drew a large knife. I laughed. He tried to dodge and discovered that he was hemmed in on all sides. The aeromancers' shield surrounded him and kept him waiting in front of me.

"You can't prove anything!"

"You should have stuck around a little longer. One of those vamps you hired to kill me talked. And Simone's friends identified you. And your brother left his DNA inside her. Sloppy, sloppy. But then, you're just an errand boy, aren't you? Leon and Blondie figured if they let you take the risks, they'd be safe. Not very bright of them to rely on an idiot like you. So, the only thing you have to decide is whether you go down alone, or you give up your girlfriend and maybe save yourself."

"She's not my girlfriend!" he practically screamed.

"Oh, my. You mean, you're not even getting laid? Are you at least letting her feed off you? I hear that feels good, but not my thing. It's supposed to feel better if you're also getting off. I knew you weren't very smart, but I really didn't think you were abetting mass murder for nothing. Surely Leon promised you something. A promotion to master when he sat on the Council? Maybe some of his sloppy seconds?"

He was within reach of my blade, and I really wasn't enjoying the game. I flicked my wrists, and the spelled sword penetrated his shield. His hand and the knife fell to the ground.

Jacob screamed, squeezing his wrist with his other hand and staring at it in horror. His shield shattered, and I kicked him in the stomach. He stumbled and fell. I stood over him, my sword point resting against his shirt just below his ribs.

"Your girlfriend, Jacob. Where is she? Last chance, or I let you bleed to death."

"Armstead Apartments! Number 36."

"Name?"

"Daniela Olinsky! Oh, God, please."

Dierdre was suddenly at my side. She grabbed his arm and cast a spell. Compressed air staunched the bleeding. She ripped the sleeve off his shirt and twisted the fabric into a tight rope.

"Named after her mother," Dierdre said to me as she tied a rough tourniquet around his wrist. "Dear Goddess, I hope you never get pissed at me."

"I'm about to throw up," I said. "What a pathetic excuse for a human being."

Several Guild security men grabbed Jacob, cast spells to immobilize him, and dragged him away.

I really was close to throwing up. I had killed a lot of vampires and werewolves, but I had never tortured any of them. The idea that someone could get pleasure from the terror that Jacob Rathske experienced was more than I wanted to think about.

Master Greenwood stepped up beside me and pulled me into his arms.

"Are you all right?"

The dam burst, and tears spilled down my face. "Not really." I buried my face in his shoulder and sobbed.

Master Olinsky and Amelia stood about ten feet away from us, but I could hear them talking to each other.

"I feel dirty," Master Olinsky said.

"It was necessary," Amelia answered her.

"I know, but damn, Amy, she's just a little girl. What we've done to her. I want to kick her grandmother's ass."

"I'll hold her for you."

Master Olinsky called Leon to the Council chambers that evening, ostensibly to discuss the openings on the Council. Dierdre and Amelia took me with them, and we found a dozen senior mages already there, scattered around the circular room. And, of course, all of the Councilors were there as well.

The veils we passed through to enter the room were like walking through molasses, and the feel of magic inside was the strongest I had ever felt. I also felt rather strange.

"The room is warded," Dierdre said, leaning close to my ear. "No magic can be performed here. It's this way in every Council room in every Guild Hall in the world. Discussions between mages with differing points of view can get quite heated, and so spells were devised to prevent bloodshed."

Rathske arrived, and took a seat near Diana. He nodded to her, and to Master Greenwood, and a couple of other older mages who I didn't know. A brief scowl crossed his features when he saw me there, but he immediately straightened his face.

"As you know," Olinsky said to the room as a whole, "we have had some very troubling events recently. We've lost some of our members, including several members of the Council. But we have finally learned the cause of our problems, and I've called you all here to share that knowledge, and to plan our course going forward."

Most of those present showed surprise, and an air of anticipation filled the room. Master Rathske pursed his lips, narrowed his eyes, and I thought I saw his shoulders hunch a little. His posture definitely conveyed tension.

"Leon Rathske," Olinsky continued, "you are officially under arrest for the crimes of using your magic to harm people and property. You are also charged with murder, rape, sedition, and abuse of your position. Before you say anything, know that we not only have physical evidence against you but also that your brother has provided testimony as to your crimes."

Rathske was sitting upright in his seat, even leaning toward Olinsky as she spoke. His hands gripped the arms of his chair so tightly that his knuckles turned white. Half a dozen of the people in the room moved toward him, and two grabbed his arms. His hands were pulled together, and handcuffs were snapped around his wrists. A silver band was snapped around his neck.

His face grew red, and then he spoke through gritted teeth, "You bloody bitch. You've always hated me, kept me from advancing. And now you've cooked up these false charges to remove me. You won't rule forever. There are more who feel like me. Mages were born to rule, not sweep up vermin to make useless humans feel safe in their beds. Someday, we will oust you and your weak-willed quislings. Our movement will survive me."

Olinsky just shook her head. "Take him away and secure him."

CHAPTER 49

I wanted in on Daniela Olinsky. That was personal.

Jacob told us that she contacted his brother sometime after the second time the demon manifested. He didn't know why she contacted Leon, or why she thought he would be amenable to joining her vendetta. But Jacob did tell us that he and Leon had been using rogues in the vampire community for years. The murders of my parents were only one of Leon's schemes, as were several bank and jewelry store robberies, both in Queen City and other regional cities.

He had also identified a dozen more Guild members who formed a group that believed in a magiocracy—a feudal-type system with mages ruling over the rest of humanity. Olinsky had them rounded up and arrested. Some of them talked freely.

Jacob did reveal that my mother's murder was an accident. Leon had planned to kill my dad, expecting that he could pick up his relationship with Mom again. She had followed my father that night, and when he was ambushed, she stepped in to help him. The null-magic entrapment had caught her, too, and the vampires weren't picky about who they killed.

Daniela's apartment was placed under surveillance from the moment Jacob spilled the beans. She had tried to contact Jacob twice, and we had let her calls go to his voicemail without response. When her attempts to contact Jacob failed, she tried to call Leon.

The dhampir had been in and out of the apartment several times since we started monitoring her. It didn't appear that she cooked, but she did visit a grocery store and brought some food home. She ate dinner at a steakhouse two nights in a row, and when security questioned the restaurant staff, they said she often ate there. She always ordered her steaks very rare.

"At least she's not dining on the local citizenry," I muttered to Dierdre when we received the report.

"The suspense is killing me," Dierdre said. "When is she going to do something?"

"Remember, her procurer is out of action. I don't think she's comfortable corralling the sacrifices by herself. I mean, I'm sure she's able, but it probably isn't much fun."

When Daniela made her move, she drove her old Chevy sedan to the seedy part of town, cruised down Colfax, and talked a young hooker into her car. They drove back to Daniela's apartment and went inside.

A few hours later, Daniella took the girl to the Convention Center. They parked, and walked around to the sculpture garden. The girl stumbled, and Daniella had to help her walk. It was pretty obvious she was drugged.

Daniella dumped the girl on the sidewalk, where she passed out. Then the dhampir began chalking her circles. The area was still closed off from traffic, and there wasn't anyone around except for the Guild personnel covertly watching.

When Daniella dragged the girl into the circle and produced a large kitchen knife, Dierdre floated me off the roof of the building. I landed just outside the outer circle.

"Hello, Daniella. We meet again," I said.

"Not you again, you stupid bitch. Why don't you go play with the vamps and leave me alone?"

"You're more fun. And the bounty on you is far larger than any vamp. Magical dhampir are in a class of their own. But before I take your head, I am curious about why you have such bitterness toward your sister. Jealous?"

She snorted a laugh. "Miss prissy master mage? She inherited everything, and what did I get? Raised in a vampire nest by a father who drank my blood. Yeah, just a little jealous. But she isn't the belle of the ball now, is she? The norms see what magic can do. Not just a little entertainment. I can't believe the idiots let you lord over them instead of tossing you all in a pit and lighting you on fire."

"My, you *are* bitter, aren't you? Well, game's over. You have two choices, turn yourself in, or go down fighting. My guess is that you're not much of a fighter."

She brandished the chef's knife and stalked toward me. When she got close enough, I struck with my sword. As before, my sword seemed to slide off her peculiar shield. She closed and struck with her knife, but it didn't penetrate my shield.

I pulled threads from the ley line and began to wrap them around her. She tried twice more to stab me, then whipped around and tried to run, but tripped over the girl she planned to sacrifice, and fell to the ground.

I pounced, standing astraddle of her body, and drove my *katana* straight down with both hands. There was resistance, but the sword penetrated her shield, and drove through to the ground. She struggled, waving her arms and legs like a pinned bug.

Backing away, I watched her, unable to tear my eyes away. I tried to tell myself she wasn't human, but her blood was human red, and as her movements slowed, she died. Only the second human I'd ever killed. It was different than putting an end to a vampire or a lycanthrope.

And then Dierdre and the other mages were there. Dierdre pulled me away, pushed me into the back seat of a car, and someone drove me away.

CHAPTER 50

To my surprise, Master Olinsky announced her resignation from the Council a week later. Master Greenwood was voted to the role of Council Chairman.

Olinsky admitted that she had known of Leon Rathske's political leanings, and that he was a pedophile, but judged that he was basically harmless. She prevented his ascension to the Council and placed him in charge of the bounty program. That was motivated in part by a desire to keep him away from the Guild's students.

It also turned out that she knew of her half-sister, and had even met her once. Her refusal to acknowledge Daniela, or consider sponsoring her as a member of the Guild, was one of the things that fueled Daniela's hatred. The demon summonings started soon after that, but Master Olinsky swore that she never connected her sister to the demon.

I tried to talk Mrs. O'Reilly into letting Lisa and Caro take my apartment, but she wouldn't do it. The girls were too young. But then Diana Olinsky and Dierdre announced that they were building a boarding school for non-magical children who were either orphaned or otherwise on their own. A place for street kids to get off the street without going into Social Services' foster care system.

A couple of weeks after the terror trio got their just rewards, Amelia came to see me in my room at the Guild Hall. I invited her in and made tea. She was my first guest. Dierdre had been in the place several times, but her visits were more like a whirlwind, getting me dressed appropriately for some occasion.

"Dierdre tells me that you have an apartment, other than this one," Amelia said.

"Yes, it's where I was living when Master Greenwood sort of discovered me."

"Well, now that we have the demon issue solved, we don't think you have time to play tracker anymore. Kaitlyn, your potential is so great, and you're getting started somewhat late with your training. We think you should give up the apartment."

I shrugged. "This place is actually much nicer. Or do you plan to move me out to the Farm with the other students?"

She shook her head. "Yes, you can keep this room, but we were thinking of also giving you a room in the Master's mansion. It would make it much more convenient for me to mentor you. The other option is, Dierdre has offered a room at her place in Evergreen."

Although a bus ran out to Evergreen, it was thirty miles from the city. At least at the Master's, I could use my bike to get around. There was a mall and multiple different stores within an hour's walk.

I took a deep breath. "I'm not sure I'm ready to join his household."

Amelia looked at me in surprise and burst out laughing. "If I get your meaning, that isn't what is being offered. Believe me, we see you as a young person that needs more structure, education, and training."

More structure. That sounded a bit ominous. "So, how much would my freedom be restricted?"

"Not much at all. You'll be free to come and go, although we will ask that you let us know where you're going and when you expect to be back. I think that's reasonable if we're going to take responsibility for you."

I had spent the past two years bitter that no one seemed to feel I was worth taking responsibility for. I nodded. It felt like I had found a family, and I couldn't stop the smile I felt growing on my face.

"Okay."

The following day, I accompanied Jodi to her testing. It was done in the same room at the mansion as mine had been. The truthsayer, Carpenter, was absent. Amelia took his place, along with Master Olinsky and Master Greenwood.

I sat beside Jodi as they questioned her. After the first couple of minutes, she reached out and took my hand under the table. The questions and monitoring using electrodes and instruments took only a couple of hours.

After that, we all piled into the Master's Range Rover and drove down to the Guild Hall. From there, we transported out to the Farm.

I knew Jodi was powerful, but the expressions on Amelia's and the Masters' faces as they put her through her paces were almost comical. She was able to do about fifty percent of the pyromancer exercises they assigned her. Several of their expendable buildings needed rebuilding by the time they called a halt.

Olinsky then took us to one of the girls' dormitories, and showed Jodi her room.

"I won't be living in town?"

"Our school and training facilities are here," Master Olinsky explained. "But you're not a prisoner here. You can come to town on weekends."

"And where will I stay there?"

"At my house." Master Greenwood knelt down so his face was even with hers. "Jodi, you're going to be living the same way Dierdre did when she was your age."

"But, the school's here," Jodi said, confusion obvious on her face. "Amelia said something once about me being able to take classes at the university. Can I still do that?"

The Master's face cracked. He reached out and pulled her into a hug. A tear ran down his cheek. "Of course you can. You can study anything you want."

Amelia also replaced Dierdre as my mentor. I was informed that I would be given a full schedule of study including mathematics, chemistry, physics, biology, English, and German—in addition to the intensive study of magic.

"Why do I need to learn German?" I asked.

"Because you'll need it when you go to university," Amelia answered.

"University? What university?"

"Zurich University. That's where my grandfather lives, and he's agreed to take you as his apprentice."

"I'm confused. I'm going to study magic at Zurich University?"

Amelia grinned. "Not exactly. We're hoping you decide to study medicine. It's important that a magical healer also be a doctor. But you're free to study anything you want."

"Okay. Now I'm more confused. I'm going to be a doctor? Why?" If she told me I was going to be an astronaut or President I wouldn't be more surprised.

"Kaitlyn, my grandfather, like you, is a spirit mage. He can control any kind of magic, but the one he considers most important is healing. You'll learn many other things, as well, never fear. But there is a lot of knowledge we need to stuff into that empty head of yours before that happens."

She handed me a piece of paper. "Those are your assignments for tomorrow. Ten o'clock sharp."

The list filled the paper with a dozen bullet points. I knew the math problems alone would take me a couple of hours.

<hr />

My room—or should I say suite—at the Greenwood mansion was something out of a TV show. Rich girl's rooms. I could probably live in one of the closets and rent the rest out. But what I enjoyed the most was the back garden, and one of the gardeners was friendly, and kind, and answered every question I asked. With summer coming, I sat out there a lot, reading, or just admiring the view.

But I also found myself increasingly spending time at the Guild Hall, and slept in my room there most nights. In spite of being in a building with hundreds of people at all times, my room there felt more private than when I was at the mansion.

So, when the intercom spoke to me one day, it about scared me out of my mind. I had forgotten it existed.

"Kaitlyn Dunne. Master Greenwood requests your presence at his home for dinner this evening. Please acknowledge."

"Uh, yeah. Okay. Tell him I'll be there." I hated talking to a box on the wall. Somehow, it seemed more sinister, less personal than talking to a box I held in my hand, but I really couldn't explain how.

It would take me at least an hour and a half to get there—a bus from Carlisle Square, then a transfer, and the last two miles on foot. But he—and Dierdre and Amelia—would expect me to dress "appropriately."

I could, of course, set out immediately and change clothes at the mansion. My wardrobe was insane, split between two locations, and I'd never worn half of it. With a sigh, I opted for a pair of sand-colored wide-leg trousers and a matching jacket with a black silk shirt. And what Amelia called sensible shoes.

With at least an hour on the bus ahead of me, I grabbed one of my textbooks—I didn't even bother to check which one, I was behind in everything. Who knew that they actually taught some useful stuff in ninth and tenth grades? Especially the science stuff.

By the time I reached the Master's house, I was somewhat more versed in German grammar. I still didn't understand why they capitalized so many words. It was like they were shouting at me.

As I trudged along the driveway toward the side door—I had learned that the front door was for guests only—I glimpsed someone carrying a large bowl of something from the kitchen to the back garden. I thought of the garden parties I'd seen portrayed on TV at English manor houses in Victorian times and smiled. The Master was old enough to have lived in such times.

When I walked into the kitchen, the cook saw me, and with a horrified look on her face shooed me out.

"We're busy in here, and you'll mess up your nice clothes. Dierdre is in the back."

She wasn't quite quick enough to keep me from seeing the large, lavish cake. And as I walked around to the garden, it hit me—mere seconds before I rounded a neatly trimmed cedar tree and walked into the dinner party.

"Happy birthday!" About twenty people cried out. I couldn't believe it. I didn't think anyone knew or cared. The Master and his household, Dierdre, Amelia, Master Olinsky, Scott from the dojo, Loretta Lighthorse, Jodi, Caro, Lisa, and half a dozen more street kids I knew were there.

The cook and one of her helpers appeared behind me, carrying the cake, and set it on the table in the garden. It said, "Happy Birthday Katy/Kaitlyn" with a large "17".

I couldn't hold back the tears, and I couldn't hold back the smile.

***

At the time of writing of this book, there were an estimated 700,000 unaccompanied homeless youth between 13-17 living on the streets in the U.S. Another 450,000 were living in foster homes.

If you enjoyed **Demon Dance and Other Disasters**, I hope you will take a few moments to leave a brief review on the site where you purchased your copy. It helps to share your experience with other readers. Potential readers depend on comments from people like you to help guide their purchasing decisions. Thank you for your time!

Get updates on new book releases, promotions, contests and giveaways! Sign up for my newsletter.

VISIT MY WEBSITE OR FACEBOOK PAGE

https://brkingsolver.com/

https://www.facebook.com/brkingsolver

BOOKS BY BR KINGSOLVER

A Spirit Mage's Journey
Demon Dance and Other Disasters

The Crossroads Chronicles
Family Ties
Night Market
Ruby Road

Wicklow College of Arcane Arts
The Gambler Grimoire
The Revenge Game

The Rift Chronicles
Magitek
War Song
Soul Harvest

Rosie O'Grady's Paranormal Bar and Grill
Shadow Hunter
Night Stalker
Dark Dancer
Well of Magic
Knights Magica

The Dark Streets Series

Gods and Demons

Dragon's Egg

Witches' Brew

The Chameleon Assassin Series

Chameleon Assassin

Chameleon Uncovered

Chameleon's Challenge

Chameleon's Death Dance

Diamonds and Blood

The Telepathic Clans Saga

The Succubus Gift

Succubus Unleashed

Broken Dolls

Succubus Rising

Succubus Ascendant

Other books

I'll Sing for my Dinner

Trust

Printed in Great Britain
by Amazon